HARVEST FROM A SMALL VINEYARD

HARVEST
FROM A SMALL
VINEYARD

A NOVEL BY
Caryl Porter

Harold Shaw Publishers
Wheaton, Illinois

Sections of this book, some in slightly different form, have appeared in the following publications: *Abba, A Journal of Prayer; Christian Century; The Family Album; The Los Angeles Times; Spirit and Life; Standard; Together*

ISBN 0-87788-342-4

Cover illustration © 1992, Donna Nelson

Book design by Ron Kadrmas

Library of Congress Cataloging-in-Publication Data

Porter, Caryl.
    Harvest from a small vineyard / Caryl Porter. — Rev. ed.
      p. cm.
    ISBN 0-87788-342-4
    I. Title.
    PS3566.0642H37 1992
    813'.54—dc20   91-24215
                                             CIP

---

99 98 97 96 95 94 93 92

10 9 8 7 6 5 4 3 2 1

to my husband,
Alvin Porter,
with love

On this gold autumn day, I look out of the window of my workroom toward our back hill. The hill frequently offers surprises of one kind and another. It rises steeply behind a cement block wall. Our California oaks lean against the sky. Today it is clear, the morning all blue and gold, spiced with the red, salmon, white of oleander blossoms.

This morning's surprise comes quietly. I see two deer, a buck, and a doe, emerging from the brush. They look straight into my eyes as I, motionless, watch them from behind my window. For a moment, before they move away on their elegant slim legs, we look at each other. Have they been drawn by the water, the sprinklers on the hill? This has been a long season of heat and drought. All of us, people and animals, long for the comfort and restorative power of water. Living water.

And we long for more than that.

As the deer longs for the water-brooks,
so longs my soul for you, O God.

The parallel is inescapable, especially in this autumn of seasons. I am restless, filled with longing, with vague homesickness, although I am at home.

In his book, *Heaven, The Heart's Deepest Longing*, Peter Kreeft says, "What you will find in your heart is not heaven but a picture of heaven, a silhouette of heaven, a heaven-shaped shadow, a longing unsatisfied by anything on earth."

The moments that, just for an instant, impinge on that "heaven-shaped shadow" are the ones that nourish, that bring the heart up into the throat, that cause sudden tears for no rational reason. They are the cosmic surprises. Sometimes they come in the shape of deer, sometimes as people.

Sometimes they take hold of us during music. Sometimes they confront us as poems, as a carving, a painting. Sometimes they come as memories.

However they come, they change our lives.

So it is time. It is autumn, the time for harvesting. Mine is a small vineyard. One woman's life. But I must begin the harvest and gather into orderly shapes the fruits, the gifts, the glimpses, the positives and the negatives, so that I may give thanks.

It is time.

A few days before Christmas the telephone rings and it is my brother Martin. I never know when to expect these calls. Sometimes a year goes by and we do not talk together, I do not know where he is. I am not even sure what he looks like now. Does his face still have its private, closed look? I cannot picture it. Now we speak in generalities for a few moments.

Soon, however, comes a specific. "Do you remember," he asks abruptly, "the year I got that mouse for Christmas?"

I remember. It was when our father was rector of a small parish in South Dakota. Christmas gifts would arrive from well-meaning strangers. We called them the Missionary Boxes.

On that particular Christmas when Martin was about eight and I five years older, I had a gift of books. Martin's gift was elaborately wrapped. He loved opening packages. It took him a long time to untie the ribbon, to remove the paper so it did not tear. He sat on the floor, his best white shirt coming out of his trousers, his black bow tie askew. A corner of adhesive tape was peeling away from the bandage on his knee.

He carefully took the cover off the box and lifted out a tin mouse. The head was dented, one of the ears missing. A key, bent and twisted, inserted into a slot in the back showed that once the mouse had been able to run.

I saw the glance that passed between my parents. Mother looked dismayed, Father angry.

Max, our old cat, was curled up on a pile of wrappings under the tree. I took the mouse from Martin and shoved it toward Max. He sniffed at it, pawed it gently, rose, and stalked away disdainfully.

I laughed.

Martin went to his room, white and silent.

Now his voice comes to me again on the telephone. "Do you remember?" he asks.

"Of course I remember."

"You thought it was funny." His voice holds years of accusation, of bitterness.

"No," I tell him. "I laughed but it wasn't because I thought it was funny. I thought it was awful. I still do."

"You all thought it was funny. I was always the butt of somebody's foul joke."

"It may have seemed that way," I tell my brother, this man who can't hear me. "I can see how it must have seemed to you."

"It didn't seem that way. It was that way. And there's something else."

"What else?" I am apprehensive. The atmosphere is ominous.

"How old was I the first time I was so sick? That winter on the island?"

"Three or four," I say. "I don't remember exactly."

But I remember exactly the feeling in the house; the anxiety, the fear. I remember my mother's strained face, my father's long, solitary hours in the cold church. I remember my own promise to the one in the stained glass window above the altar, the one I often talked with. *You can do anything to me, but don't let him die.* Oh, I remember.

Martin says, his voice flat and cold, "I'll tell you something. You didn't want me to get well. Not any of you. None of you ever cared about me. And when I did get well, you felt guilty because you hadn't wanted me to. So you've punished me all these years because I didn't die."

Now I know what it means, that phrase, *My blood ran cold*. Time stops and I am caught in a vast, icy space.

At last he speaks. "Julie? Are you there?"

Somehow I manage to answer. "Yes. I'm here."

"It's true, you know." He is convinced.

My own voice is unsteady. "You're wrong. You're terribly wrong. I can see that you believe it, but you're wrong. We were all terrified for fear you wouldn't get well. I . . ." But I can't tell him about my bargain with the one in the window. He wouldn't believe me.

He speaks across the wasteland. "I know what I know. I've always known it. You can't fool a child, even one as young as I was. He picks up vibrations."

"Oh, Martin," I begin, thinking of that little boy lying in his bed all changed, hearing him cry with pain. "Oh, Martin . . ." But my voice breaks.

He relents a bit. "I suppose I shouldn't dump all this garbage on you just before Christmas." Now he speaks half seriously, half in irony. "Well, deck the halls. Peace on earth. And all that."

"Yes," I say. But he has hung up.

I am cold, so cold that I shake with the chill of my brother's words. "In the bleak midwinter." The carol sifts like snow into my consciousness. "In the bleak midwinter." In what bleak winter has Martin been wandering alone, all these years of our lives?

The hours, the days avalanche, and I struggle through them to Christmas Eve. Todd and I go to St. Paul's at midnight. My heart does not lift at the scent of pine, at the sight of crimson berries, at the sound of carols. Even when I hear the words, "And there were in the same country shepherds, keeping watch . . ." my heart will not sing at the coming of this blessed night.

3

Kneeling, I fight for inner silence. I gather together all the lifelong hurts: Martin's despair and anger, my father's pride, my mother's disappointments. My own failures. I gather them and, trying to pray, I offer up the pain.

Take it. Take it all and bless it. Give it back to me to bear, if you must. But strengthen me. And in your own time, heal us. Heal us all.

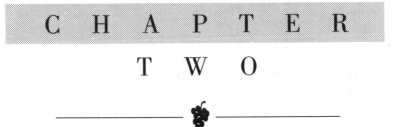

CHAPTER
TWO

I cannot seem to cast off the darkness that has surrounded me since Martin's call, in spite of all the festivity of the Christmas season. So on the twelfth day of Christmas, the Feast of the Epiphany, the day of the Three Kings, Todd and I make a pilgrimage.

Now we stand at the top of the world looking down toward the ocean. It is, of course, not really the top of the world. We stand at the top of a mountain overlooking the Pacific Ocean. We have come to a retreat house for a weekend of reflection and renewal. A soft wind blows, birds call, the sun is out after a hard rain.

The monastery is operated by the brothers of the Order of the Holy Cross. We have been welcomed into the structure of their daily life. We attend their services if we wish. We eat our meals with them and we observe, if we can, their Great Silence.

Just now we have finished breakfast, a silent meal. Brother Luke, in his white habit, comes to stand by us. With his neat beard and classic face, he resembles a young St. Francis. He is carrying a baby. It is an unexpected sight. The baby tugs at Brother Luke's beard, and they both laugh. The Great Silence is over.

I ask, "Will you tell us about the baby?"

"He's the son of our new cook." Brother Luke runs a finger along the baby's cheek. "This young family came to us recently and we hired the baby's father. They are staying with us until they can find a house to rent."

"You'll miss the baby when they leave, won't you?" I ask Brother Luke.

"It's been interesting to have them here," he answers. "One could argue, of course, that the baby is a distraction. But I wonder. How much will he absorb, even so young? What will his memories be?"

What, indeed? My own dark memories remain with me just now, in this time of my brother's recollecting. "I think I'll go to the chapel for a while," I say to Todd when Brother Luke and the baby have left us. "I need to be alone. Do you mind?"

"Of course not. I'll go to the library and read." He studies me. "Things are going to be all right." His kind eyes, his concern and understanding remain among the treasured constants of my life.

I put my hand against his cheek. "Thanks." He goes to the library and I go to the chapel. I sit down and idly look out the window that opens to a patio. Giant cactus plants grow beside roses and geraniums. Great boulders rise in free-form patterns among the plants. Looking past them I see the ocean below and two boats, like toys in a child's pond.

In the tiny side chapel a votive candle glows in a glass container. One of the brothers kneels at the prie-dieu for a moment and then leaves as silently as he has come.

Sitting alone in the chapel I let pain wash over me. All through Christmas I carried the despair of my brother's residual griefs, the depths of his winter dark. Now I face the darkness, his and mine, for they are intertwined. We are parted, we who journeyed together through the early years of our lives.

I am caught in silence and I give myself over to it, opening my mind to whatever comes. Remembrance of this morning's Eucharist comes, and words from one of the prayers. "In the Mystery of the Word made flesh you have caused a new light to shine in our hearts."

Flame burns in a hanging lamp. Outside, light glints on the ocean far below. Sturdy cacti lift toward heaven. On the altar, the cross lifts toward eternity.

I realize that I have been holding my breath. The clock in the hall chimes the half-hour. A baby laughs somewhere. I slowly return to now. Soon I will go to Todd, and he and I will return to the world below, our world that makes its daily demands upon us.

But in these last moments I have committed myself to another journey. I lean away from the dark, toward a new light.

CHAPTER
THREE

The old photograph shows a child of about three bundled up in a sweater, hood, and mittens. She sits in a little box on runners, a homemade sled, with a blanket covering her legs and lap. The sled is being pulled by a middle-aged man who wears overcoat, gloves, and a fedora. The child and the man smile, squinting a bit against the sun. The shadow of a long skirt suggests that a woman took the picture.

I was the child. My father pulled the sled, and my mother took the picture. On the back of the snapshot, in my mother's small, neat handwriting are the words Julie Erlich, 38 months. We lived in a midwestern college town where my German-born father taught philosophy and German literature.

I remember that winter. The memories are my earliest clear ones. I recall flickering moments before, but I truly remember that winter. I can see the rose color of my warm wraps, the ones my mother had knit. I can see the hard-packed snow around us, the sun glinting on it with bits of light too elusive for me to catch and hold.

I can see my parents: my mother's blue dress, the one I liked best; my father's smooth bald head with the fringe of curly hair around the back. I hear my mother saying, "Karl, really!" with just a hint of laughter in her voice when he asked me to recite for his friends some sentences he had taught me to say. More than half a century later I remember those words:

"My father desires me to cultivate a polysyllabic enunciation. Polysyllabic enunciation is one of my father's eccentricities."

He would shout with laughter when I said it all perfectly, toss me in the air, and then catch me and hold me close to him. I remember the texture of his cheek when I kissed him, smooth and smelling of something spicy.

I didn't know then, of course, that year when I was riding in a sled, and being tossed in the air by a laughing father, that an Archduke had been murdered a few years before, halfway across the world. Many things changed after that. Our lives changed, too.

Although my father was an American citizen, he had a German name. He read to me in German sometimes. He taught me the grace that I always said before meals:

Komm, Herr Jesu, sei unser Gast, und segne was Du uns bescheret hast.

Our own children have always said that grace in English, and now our daughter's daughter uses it, too:

Come, Lord Jesus, be our Guest, and bless what Thou hast given us.

That is now. But on a Sunday long ago I sat at lunch beside my mother, feeling shy in the presence of our important guests. The president of the college was there, large, stern, and quiet. His wife was quiet, too, but she smiled at me across the table.

I was in my own place. I still have my silver cup, dented from teething, and my small fork and spoon, engraved with my name. I said grace, as I always did, in German.

The next day my father was dismissed from the college.

I do not remember that. I have been told most of it and the rest I put together for myself over the years, as children do.

So, at the age of forty-three, with a wife and a small child, in a land suddenly turned hostile, my father started over. He went to seminary. *Semina:* seed. Seed: new beginning. Seminary: a nurturing place for the Word.

I remember my father, all through my childhood, singing the choral theme from the Beethoven Ninth, bumbling like a great bee: *Alle Menschen werden Brüder.*

And he'd say, "All men are brothers, *liebchen*. But sometimes they forget."

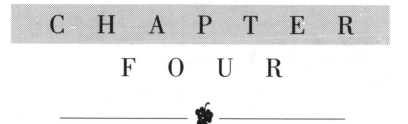

CHAPTER
FOUR

The Christmas I was five my father taught me the nativity story from St. Luke, and I said it, from memory, at the seminary Christmas Eve service for children. Every time I hear the words, "And there were in the same country shepherds, keeping watch over their flocks by night," that Christmastime returns to me. I hear my father's voice. I see the light from the kerosene stove that cast shapes like a lace doily on the ceiling of my father's study.

And I see my mother sewing. She had been sewing all that winter. I liked to watch when she moved the shining needle in and out of the cloth in tiny stitches, or when she embroidered with soft, delicate colors. That winter my mother's hands would become chapped, and her fingertips would crack. Sometimes blood would stain the cloth and she would have to wash the garments even before they were finished.

I knew that those clothes, so small and white, were to be for our baby. My parents had told me that before spring I would have a brother or a sister. I thought of Thumbelisa, the tiny child in the fairy story. She was found in a tulip. So I asked my parents, "But where will you get the baby? There are no tulips in winter."

Soft, rosy color would tinge my mother's face and she would seem shy. But my father told me. "The baby grows inside your mother. Come, put your hand here. Do you feel the baby move?"

He would put my hand against the swollen part of my mother, and I could feel something moving there. My mother always seemed to be uneasy when I did this. But my father would say, "Come. Come, feel the baby move." It was quite mysterious.

One February morning I went to stay next door at my friend Bobby's house. Father carried a small suitcase with my things in it, and when he took me next door he said, "I know you will be a good child. Soon our baby will be born, and I will come and tell you. Pray to *Herr Jesu* that the baby and your mother will have a safe journey. Pray, *liebchen*."

He was very serious as he spoke, as he kissed me, and I thought he must be thinking about his first wife and their new baby. It had been very long ago, when my father was young. His wife and their baby had both died.

I wondered what I would do if my mother and this baby died. My father had told me to pray, and I did. Martin was born just before midnight, while I was asleep. When he and my mother finally came home and I went home, too, I saw my brother for the first time. He was small, but not as small as Thumbelisa. His mouth made strange motions, and he sounded like a new kitten.

My father had me sit in a chair with a pillow behind my back and a blanket over my lap. He gave me my brother, showing me how to put my hand behind his wobbly head. I touched his hand and his fingers curled around my own finger.

"Martin," I said, "I'll read to you when you are a little older. I'll tell you stories and sing to you. We'll be best friends."

"*Ja,* indeed," my father said. "Brother and sister and also friends." Then he gently took the baby from me and gave him to my mother. He knelt beside them and stroked Martin's cheek. His hand looked very large. He laid that hand, for just a moment, against my mother's face. Then he started to sing, "*Nun danket Alle Gott,*" and the whole room was full of his voice. "Now thank we all our God," he sang. Martin made little mewing noises.

"Shh, Karl," my mother said. "Not so loud."

Father laughed and stopped singing. Kneeling there, he looked at all of us. He shook his head, as if he were surprised at something.

"What is it?" my mother asked him.

"I do not understand," he said. "I do not understand how one man can be so happy."

CHAPTER

FIVE

───────────── ❦ ─────────────

My parents seldom spoke about the seminary years. They must have been almost impossibly difficult. I believe my mother's parents helped when they could. I do not remember much about that time.

I do remember that we lived in our own small house and my father tutored students, young men who came to him there. I especially liked Mr. Simon, who called me his little rabbit and who brought me a shiny yellow ball.

Sometimes, after he had attended his morning classes and given lessons to his students in the afternoon, Father would fall asleep while we were eating supper.

Mother would look worried and say, "Karl, you are working too hard."

But Father would say, "Do not worry. It will be all right. You will see. I shall study for a while now."

Bobby lived next door, and I liked to play in his yard because he had a tree house. His father taught us how to climb the ladder that led up to it, and I was never afraid. When we were in the tree house near the sky, in our own private forest, Bobby and I were in a secret world.

We thought we would be together always. We would be married, and we would find our children in tulip blossoms, like Thumbelisa. That way I would not have to leave Bobby for a while to go to the hospital, as my mother had done. We were eager to have the time come when we could go to school so that we could learn how to read. Then we could read to our children.

"Mother, read to me." I am sure those must have been my most frequently spoken words. My mother read to me every night when I was ready for bed and sometimes, when I could coax her, during the day.

She would read from *Mother Goose* and Hans Christian Andersen. Or from *Peter Rabbit* or the *Just So Stories*. I knew my favorites by heart, and I loved to read along with her. "Go to the banks of the great grey-green greasy Limpopo River, all set about with fever trees, and find out." I felt as if I had been there with the Elephant's Child.

My father, when he had time, read German poetry to me, and I loved the sound of the strange words spoken by his deep, rumbling voice.

I could hardly wait to go to school because, my parents assured me, when I had been in school awhile I would learn to read by myself. How wonderful, I thought, to be able to understand the marks on the pages, to be able to turn them into stories. Then I would be able to read to Martin when he was old enough to listen.

On that first day of school, when it finally came, my father took my picture. The enlarged snapshot shows a tall, serious child holding a book. Her hair is drawn back from her forehead and tied with a large bow. She wears a middy blouse and skirt, long white stockings, a bit wrinkled, and Buster Brown shoes. Her expression is sweetly grave. She is poised on the edge of discovery.

Our mothers walked to school with us that first morning, but after that Bobby and I walked together. I felt supremely secure with my hand in Bobby's. So it was a terrible shock to us both when, after a while, Bobby was put in one group and I in another. We could still walk to school and home again together, but we were separated for the rest of the day. I felt abandoned.

Things were not going well for me in several ways. The other children began to read words on the charts and the stories that were in our books. I could not see anything but the familiar squiggles, like those in our books at home. There was no magic transformation into words. My parents had promised that I would soon be able to read. They always kept their promises. But I could not read.

I couldn't paint neatly, either, or stay inside the lines when we colored. My mother never asked me to stay inside lines. I always had the freedom of a whole page. And I couldn't even string the beads, not the smallest ones, or recognize children I knew when they were way across the playground. I felt that there must be something wrong with me. I failed in so many ways.

At home, my parents acted so happy when they asked me, "How was school today?" that I always answered, "Fine." I didn't want to disappoint them. I would run to see Martin. He welcomed me with his wide, toothless grin and his own language of gurgling sounds. "You love me anyway, don't you?" I'd ask. And he would laugh and kick and pull my hair.

When my mother would read to me I'd say the words with her and that would make me feel better. I told my father that I was afraid I was not like the other children because I could not read yet.

"Don't worry, *liebchen*. Soon you will read. Besides, to be different is not always a bad thing. One comes to terms with it. There are compensations."

Although I did not always understand what they meant, I was glad my parents talked to me as if I were grown up. Still, sometimes I felt that I couldn't do anything right at school, and the other children laughed at me. Miss Harley would be angry then, but not with me. With them. She never made me feel different. I loved her.

One day after school she handed me a note and said, "Julie, will you please give this to your mother when you go home?"

Soon after that my parents took me to see Dr. Riley. He was very tall. He wore a white coat, and he smelled of wintergreen. He sat me in a chair and told me to hang on tight while he gave me a ride. When I was sitting quite high, on a level with his face, he asked me to put my chin on the ledge of a strange, cold machine. We played games in which I told him what I saw. He would say, over and over, "Hmmm. Uh-huh." His face was close to mine and I liked the wintergreen smell.

When he had finished, he put a pair of glasses on me, pushing them back against the bridge of my nose, fitting the bows over my ears. "Now," he said, "take a look around."

First I looked at my mother. I stared and stared. There was a little scar at the corner of her mouth. She had beautiful eyes, brightly blue, and her lashes were long. Something in the way she looked at me made me want to cry.

Then I looked at my father. His forehead had wrinkles, and tiny lines showed around his eyes. Those eyes, behind thick lenses, smiled at me, but they looked sad at the same time. I thought it very strange.

At last I said to my parents, "I didn't know you looked that way." I couldn't understand why they cried, I was so happy.

Dr. Riley cleared his throat and said, "Young lady, I can't let you take these glasses with you, but you'll have some of your own very soon. You'll need to wear glasses all your life. Your eyes can't see much without help. You'll get used to wearing glasses. You won't mind them at all. Here, have a wintergreen."

After I had my own glasses it wasn't long before words formed themselves on the pages and I was finally part of the world of books. I began to see things when I looked at them. Martin had dimples in his wrists and elbows, and he smiled at me when I talked to him. He smiled at *me*. Leaves had veins in them. So did stones. Under stones I found insects and other squirmy things, each one different from the other. Pansies had faces. I let Bobby look through my magic glasses, but they hurt his eyes.

When I would discover something new and tell my parents about it they would look at each other and sigh. Once my mother said, "Karl, how could we have been so blind?"

"How indeed?" my father said. "We had ears and did not hear, eyes and did not see."

But I could see now, and I walked among wonders.

CHAPTER
SIX

———— 🍇 ————

When my father finished his work at the seminary and was ordained, we moved to another small midwestern town where he had his first parish. I was very sad when I had to leave Bobby. But I made a friend in the new town, and her name was Beth.

At that time in my life my mother was always right. If, for example, she said, "Take your umbrella. It's going to rain," I took it and it did. If she said, "You may wear a sweater today instead of your coat," she was right. The air was warm. Once I thought I knew better than she did when she said, "Take your mittens. It's going to snow." I didn't, and it did.

So naturally I became a docile and obedient daughter. After all, what was the use of deliberately courting disaster? All went well until I was nearly eight. Then there came a moment in which I was faced with a double obedience, and I did not know which to choose.

Come right home after school. This was an understood, long-followed rule. In fact, she didn't have to say it anymore. The words stood by themselves each morning as I went out the door on my way to school, and they stood in the school hallway as I left at three thirty.

Sometimes I walked partway home with my friend Beth. One winter afternoon she said to me, "Why don't you come with me today and hear my piano lesson? Professor Mannheim won't mind."

Of course I could not consider it because of the words that hung in the air as a shield before me. When we had reached the music school where Beth had her lesson, she said casually, "Well, anyway, run up the steps with me."

They were beautifully smooth and steep, so I did. Beth rang the bell. At once the door was opened by the largest man I had ever seen. It seemed to me, bending back to look all the way up at him, he must surely be a giant. He looked like some of the pictures I had seen of Moses and Abraham, or of God's own self. His large grey eyes, set under heavy eyebrows that were the same color as his full beard, looked right into my mind. I was sure they did.

Beth said, more politely than I had ever heard her speak, "Good afternoon, Professor. I have brought Julie to hear my lesson."

Before I could speak to deny this lie, the professor said to me in his clear, commanding voice, "Come in."

What choice had I? My mother, with her ordinary mortal voice, still said, *Come right home after school.* But here was a powerful VOICE bidding me enter. If I did not, what hidden punishment might await me? Who could say? I went in.

Comforted somewhat by my self-sworn resolve never to speak to Beth again, I walked home alone at four thirty through the early twilight. I had no place to go but home, even though I tried to conjure up a spot where I might be safe and welcome. It did no good to walk slowly. That would only make me later. On the other hand, to walk quickly would mean the swifter approach of my inevitable fate. So I just walked along.

When I reached home I went straight to the room where my mother was ironing. She looked at me and said nothing. But with a burst of strength she seized me, laid me face down on the ironing board, and turned up my skirt.

When she had finished we were both exhausted and I was hurting. I managed not to cry as I told her what had happened, although my voice was not quite steady.

To my astonishment, she held me and said over and over, "I was so worried. You always come right home. I was so worried." And it was my mother who cried first as we held each other in the warmth of that winter room.

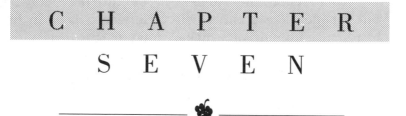

ometimes, when you are eight, the world is a lonely place if you have not yet found your way in it. Oh, I tried to find my way in still another town, another school, and I did not understand why it was that I stood outside the magic circle and everyone else stood inside it, safe and happy.

One day at school Celia spoke to me. She was the jeweler's daughter. "See my diamond ring?" Tossing her long black hair like a restless pony, she stretched out her hand. On her little finger was a thin gold band set with a diamond. Colors flashed, and I saw the sky and the green of leaves reflected in the stone.

"It's only a little one." She tossed her hair again. "Daddy says I can have a big one when I graduate from high school." I couldn't think of anything to say. Celia laughed and walked away with two of her friends.

One day after school I told my father, "I don't have any friends." I knew I was going to cry and before I realized what I was saying I sobbed, "Celia has a diamond ring."

He was sitting at the desk in his big, high-backed chair. "Come." He motioned to the chair across from him. "Come, let us read together."

He handed me a volume of German poetry. I took the heavy brown book. It smelled of old leather, and its thin pages made whispering sounds as I turned them. Through my tears I began to read aloud.

"That is good," my father said, "but turn the *r* more on your tongue. Like a bird's note." He leaned back in his chair, smoke from his pipe making fragrant streamers in the hazy air.

We would read from Goethe, or from Schiller:

Freude, schöner, Gotter-funken,
Tochter aus Elysium.

"One day you will hear it sung," my father told me. "Beethoven did it even better." He nodded his head. "Even better. You will see, Julie. You will see."

All the while my father and I read, I knew he was seeing, from some window of his memory, towers on the Rhine, the flowing river; breathing the winy, golden air of his homeland. I looked at the rows of books on the walls, thinking that my father knew everything in all of them. I wondered whether some day I would acquire all knowledge available to mankind, as he had done.

That year I was dressed mainly in other people's clothes. My mother did not enjoy sewing, but she altered things so I could wear them. She cut down a gray coat for me. It was the right length when it was finished, but it was broad in the shoulders and roomy in the sleeves. She pinned a red flower on the lapel.

The dresses I wore to school were sometimes crepe or satin. I knew I was different. The other girls knew it, too. But in the evenings my father would wind up the phonograph and put on a record. He would smile at my mother and me and say, "Now. Caruso." Then everything was all right, and we were safe there together with the music, with one another.

One spring day the girls were talking about Celia's birthday party. "Remember the clown last year?" one girl said. "I love circus parties."

"I liked the one before that when they took us all to the city, to the movies," another girl said. "What is it going to be this year, Celia?"

Celia laughed. "It's a secret," she said, looking at us as we stood in a ring around her. "It's going to be the very best one of all. I'm sending the invitations in the mail. Everybody's invitation will come in the mail."

I told my mother about it. I told her I wished I could have a new dress for the party. A real dress. A dress of my own. "What can I give Celia?" I asked my mother. What can you give a girl who has a diamond ring?

I did not get a new dress. Not really. Mother cut down a white cotton and I felt almost right in it. She made an apron and helped me embroider *Celia* on the pocket in little blue letters. I thought it was beautiful.

At school the girls talked about the invitations they had received. I heard them talking to each other, but they would change the subject when I came near. I had a sick feeling that Celia was not going to invite me. That I would be the only one not going to her party.

But she seemed friendly. She said, "I wish I could write a poem like the one you wrote. The one Miss Jameson read in class yesterday."

I hoped again. If she liked my poem, maybe she liked me, too. Three days before the party I called to my mother when I came home from school, "Mother, has my invitation come yet?"

Father answered. "Your mother is not at home, *liebchen*. She and Martin have gone out. There was no mail." As he looked at me he seemed to know what I was thinking. "Do this for me, please," he said. "I have not yet seen the new dress. Put it on, that I may see how you look in it."

I went to my room and put on the white dress. I combed my straight hair and stared at myself, solemn and pale in the shadowy mirror. Then I went downstairs and stood before my father.

"Turn around." He circled the air with his pipe. I revolved before him slowly. "Like a flower," he said. "Like a snowdrop. But are those the shoes to wear with such a dress?" I wore my brown oxfords. "Come," he said, "come." Together we went into the town.

When my mother came home I heard them talking, but I couldn't hear all they said. I was in my room with my new shoes. I had never had black patent leather slippers before. I stroked the surface of them, mirror-bright. I sniffed the fresh new smell of them. I felt them smooth and strong against the skin of my fingers, and then, princess-like on my feet. For my father I would have walked on swords, like the little mermaid. But in my new shoes there were only shafts of love.

On the day of the party my invitation still had not come. That Saturday afternoon was balmy with spring. I put on my white dress and my new shoes and sat on the back porch to wait for the mailman. Celia's package was beside me. My mother came out and stood with me.

"Do you suppose I will ever have a diamond ring?" I asked her. I took her hand, the one with the ring on it, and looked into the diamond. It was smaller than Celia's, and I could not see the myriad colors I had seen in Celia's ring; only a hint of red, a shadow of blue.

Then I saw the mailman walk past the corner. I went inside and watched from the hall window. He didn't even pause. He walked right by our house. And then I knew for sure.

I went up to my room and shut the door. Tearing the wrapping off Celia's apron, I crumpled it into a ball and threw it on the floor. I took off my white dress and put on my Saturday clothes. I started to take off my new shoes, but then the tears came. I lay on my bed with my face in the pillow and I cried for a long time. My throat hurt, and it was hard to breathe. After a while, though, the tears stopped. I smoothed out the apron, washed my face, and went down to the back porch again.

Soon my father came out and placed a bowl of soapy water beside me. He laid a piece of an old woolen mitten on the step. I had worn those mittens the year I was three. My mother had knit them. Then he put a wooden bubble pipe on my lap. I looked at it and held it against my face. The wood was smooth and tan and it touched me comfortably like my father's hand.

I dipped the pipe into the soapsuds and blew a family of small bubbles that flew away on the soft wind. The bubble pipe tasted woody and tart, faintly tinged with soap. Holding the woolen mitten on my left hand, I began to blow a large bubble. Evenly letting out my breath in tiny wisps of air, I watched it grow. There were little windows in it. When it was ripe, I flicked it carefully from the bowl of my pipe to the piece of wool and held it while it quivered and shimmered. There would never again be one just like it. I made it myself, and when it left me it would go where all bubbles go.

As I looked at it, just before it burst, I saw the most lovely colors. I saw the sky and the budding trees. I saw the back door of my house, and although I did not see my parents, I knew they were there. I saw all the fragile wonders of the world. And when at last my bubble burst, I felt cool and gentle moisture on my cheek.

CHAPTER
EIGHT

❧

One day the mailman delivered a letter from the bishop. I saw Mother look at Father anxiously while he read it.

When he had finished reading he said, "So. We move again."

"Where?" my mother asked.

"We go to an island. An island in Lake Michigan. Come. I show you."

He showed us a map of Michigan, and there was the island, a tiny dot in the blue water. The place that was to be my true home.

The island shaped my life. Like a child in a tapestry I moved among threads of gold, threads of gray: the warp of joy, the woof of grief. The tapestry was filled with the sweetness of surprise. I was forever on the verge of discovery. Something? Someone? A Presence? The Presence assumed various disguises: water, people, birds, trees. All things had their season, and all things, even sorrow, seemed inevitable and right.

I cannot explain with my intellect the pervasive importance and fascination of the island. It is not a pragmatic problem. Enough that the island, lost to me more than half a century ago, remains an archetype. I have never left it. It has never left me.

"Don't ever go back," people say to me; those who have visited my island in recent years. "Don't go back. It has changed. You wouldn't recognize it."

But I do go back. In waking and in dreaming I return. The island is the place where I discovered the God of surprises, the God of the unexpected. How often the parables warn us to be ready. Children are ready. Ready to suspend disbelief, to accept the unacceptable, to respond to the mysterious.

The island, real enough in time and place, its special geography transformed by memory, has become my personal Eden. I knew it intimately. The cedar forest, mysterious in snow, inhabited by cardinals swift as flame; early wildflowers hiding in moist underwood, their faint scent barely rising above the rich, pungent aroma of the earth itself. The living earth. And embracing everything, the lake, alive and shining. All these were parts of my book of hours.

The surprises of Eden were part of my life, as well. One night I had been asleep. Wakened by voices downstairs, I lay drowsily floating in and out of dream. I caught words and disjointed phrases. I recognized my parents' voices, and I heard the voices of strangers.

Then my mother was beside me, saying my name. "Wake up, dear. Come, wake up. We need you."

I got up and put my arms into the sleeves of the robe my mother held for me, sleepily put on my slippers, and we went downstairs together. Father, in his pajamas and robe, was holding his prayer book and his stole; the white one with the golden cross embroidered on the back by my mother.

"Ah," he said when he saw me, "here you are, Julie. Do not be afraid. Come, stand with your mother. There, so."

He kissed the cross on the back of his stole. Then he put it around his neck. Now he was not so much my father as God's servant. He had explained that to me. Standing before him were a man and woman I had never seen before. The man looked pale and worried. The woman was pale, too, but she seemed calm. She smiled at me. She looked at the man the way my mother sometimes looked at my father when she thought no one was watching.

Speaking to my mother and me, Father said, "Dearly beloved, we are gathered here in the sight of God to join together this man and this woman . . ."

When they were truly married my father said some words of his own to them. "David and Margaret, I place you in God's keeping for this life and the life to come." He made the sign of the cross over them. I shivered.

He took off his stole then and asked Mother and me to sign our names on the marriage certificate. Just as I had finished signing my name as a witness of this marriage in the deep night, someone knocked on our door. It was Mr. Humbolt, the one policeman on our island. My father greeted him. Mother took me back upstairs to bed.

"Why is Mr. Humboldt here?" I asked my mother. "Did Father do something wrong?"

"No. He did nothing wrong. This is one of the things we do not talk about with other people. It is a confidence we do not break. Do you understand?"

"Yes, Mother."

"Good." She kissed me. "Now go back to sleep."

That night remains a mystery. But I remember the feelings that surrounded it. I felt secure. My parents wouldn't do anything wrong. They had told me that God uses people to do his work, even though sometimes it seems strange. And, they had told me, even though there are times when we long to know why strange things happen, we may not always find out.

Surprises, mysteries, questions without answers; I was introduced to them on the island. Have not such things always been a part of Eden?

I did not fully understand about Stevie, either. He came to live with us for a while. He was taller than Father and his voice was deep. But he acted as though he were about the same age as my brother, Martin. Perhaps even younger. Martin often tried patiently to explain things to Stevie.

Stevie was gentle and good natured. His eyes looked as if they didn't quite know us, even when I was sure he did. His coarse hair stuck up in tufts on his head. His arms and legs looked as if they were too long for the rest of him. He shuffled his feet along in the old slippers he liked to wear in the house, and I could always hear him coming.

He loved to walk on the beach with Martin and me, gathering shells, watching the gulls soar, listening to them cry. He tried to imitate the sounds they made and he flapped his long, thin arms like wings as he tried to fly. I thought he'd like to be able to soar away with those free, white birds.

Once we found a dead gull on the sand. Stevie stroked it and said over and over, "Poor, poor, poor," while tears ran down his face. He carried the bird home, and we helped him bury it under the pear tree.

"Why is Stevie the way he is?" I asked my father that day. "He can't read or write. Martin can do more things than Stevie can, and he's only four."

"We do not understand why he is as he is," Father told me. "He looks like a man but he acts like a child."

"Does that make him unhappy?" I remembered Stevie's tears as he spoke to the dead gull.

"I do not believe that he is often unhappy," Father said. "He has a sunny nature, and you and Martin are good companions for him. There was a time, long ago, when people cherished those like Stevie, cherished and protected them, and felt blessed by their presence. Did you know?"

"Why?" I thought of the people who looked at Stevie out of the corners of their eyes when we'd meet on the beach. They would look at each other and raise their eyebrows. Then they would take their children's hands and hurry past us.

And I thought of Stevie's sister who didn't like him. The day his parents and sister brought him to live with us we all sat together at our round dining-room table and Mother served a cake she had baked that morning. It was white with chocolate frosting.

I saw Stevie carefully take the frosting off his cake and pile it in a heap on the side of his plate. Then he began to eat his cake.

"Saving your frosting, Stevie?" his sister asked. I didn't like the way her voice sounded.

Stevie smiled his wide, loose smile and nodded.

"Stevie." His father sounded angry. "When will you learn to eat like a man?"

While Stevie was looking at his father, Stevie's sister took his frosting, in one quick motion, and she ate it. When Stevie looked back at his plate he was puzzled. He looked all around, but he couldn't find his chocolate frosting. He began to cry.

"Dumbie," his sister muttered. "Crazy old dumbie."

Thinking of these things, I asked my father again, "Why?"

"Because," Father said softly, "people like Stevie are the innocent ones. They dwell in a kingdom close to God and they are perfect in his sight. This is what I believe, but I do not know why Stevie is as he is. I do not know."

Surprises, mysteries, questions without answers.

The window of the fishermen in the little church on the island appears in my dreams, too. Often it seemed to me, as I watched sunlight pour through the colored glass, that the men in the window were alive. They might speak to me at any moment and tell me wonderful secrets.

Once when I stood in the cathedral at Chartres, breathing in the light that illuminates those windows, I closed my eyes against their glory. There, an afterimage on my retinas, was the window of the fishermen. One does not lose one's earliest taste of heaven.

CHAPTER
NINE

❦

Miss Randolph was organist in our small island church. She coaxed music out of an old, recalcitrant pump organ. I used to go into the church when she was practicing and listen while she played the hymns for Sunday and other pieces of music that raised in me responses I did not understand.

She was thin and plain and her dresses were always brown or gray. No color showed in her face, which was also thin and plain. But the colors of the music she played! They blended with the colors that leapt and played on the walls near the stained glass windows. I was entranced.

One day when she was leaving the church she saw me there in the pew and stopped to speak to me. I felt embarrassed, as if I had been eavesdropping. But she did not seem surprised to see me there.

"Good morning," she said, speaking to me just as if I were an adult.

"Good morning, Miss Randolph." I stood as my mother had taught me to do when an older person spoke to me.

"Have you been listening to the music?" she asked.

"Yes, ma'am."

"Did you enjoy it?"

"Oh yes, ma'am."

"Would you like to learn to play the piano and the organ?"

Such a thought had never occurred to me, and I did not know how to answer. I had assumed that the power to make music was reserved for adults. So I just stared at her.

She looked at me calmly and then said, "Let us go and speak with your mother."

We went next door to my house. I opened the door and called, "Mother, Miss Randolph is here."

My mother came, wiping her hands on her apron. "Miss Randolph, how nice to see you. Please come in."

Miss Randolph said, without preamble, "It is time for Julie to begin piano lessons. May she start tomorrow morning at ten?"

I looked at my mother. She was surprised. I knew that. Her eyes widened slightly and she didn't answer right away.

Miss Randolph said, "I charge twenty-five cents a lesson, and Julie may earn hers by doing various tasks for me. It will be an equitable solution."

I had no idea what she meant but I liked the sound of it.

My mother said, "Thank you, Miss Randolph. She will be at your house at ten tomorrow."

I felt that these two adults were sealing my future in some way that I understood only faintly. When Miss Randolph left I said to my mother, "I didn't know I could learn how to play. I thought only grownups could do that."

"I used to play, when I was a girl." My mother's tone was matter-of-fact.

It was as if she told me that she used to arrange the lights in the heavens. Or that she caused the winds to blow. My mother, with her hands always red from wash water or chapped and bleeding in the cold weather? My mother had been able to make music?

"You never told me."

She sighed. "It was a long time ago."

I went to the porch swing and sat there wondering. I looked at my hands. They were hot and sticky. The nails were short and uneven where I had chewed them. How could these hands learn to make music come from the keys? How could I learn to read music from books as Miss Randolph did? Would all that happen tomorrow? After my lesson would I be able to play as she did?

The next morning I woke early. I went to the church and looked at the organ. I saw the black and white keys and the knobs with markings on them, like secret codes.

Then I went to the basement Sunday school room where the piano was. I sat on the bench and touched a key lightly with the index finger of my right hand. No sound. I pressed harder. I heard the sound it made. I pressed two keys at the same time and then with both hands I pressed all the keys I could manage. The sound was not music. I was sure of that.

At breakfast I asked my mother, "Where did Miss Randolph learn to make music?"

"I don't know. She's never mentioned that."

"Is she married?"

"No."

"Is it time to go yet?"

"No. Not yet."

"May I wear my blue dress?"

"Yes. And be sure to wash your hands again."

It seemed hours before it was actually time to go. When I reached Miss Randolph's house I rang the doorbell. I heard it chime faintly inside the house.

Miss Randolph opened the door. She wore one of her brown dresses. "Good morning," she said.

"Good morning, Miss Randolph."

She led me to the cool, dim room where the piano was. Everything looked tidy. Chairs sat primly as if they had always been in their own places. A green love seat looked stiff and hard and slippery. On a small polished table stood a green vase full of peacock feathers.

"Sit there, please." Miss Randolph pointed to the piano bench. I sat there and she sat on a chair beside me. "I want you to think about what I shall tell you. I want you to try to remember everything I say. Will you do that?"

"Yes, Miss Randolph." I knew that she was wise. I felt as if I were on the verge of a great discovery. My heart began to beat quickly and I resolved not to forget anything.

"Music is as orderly as the universe itself," she said. "It is full of beauty and precision. It never disappoints one, if one is faithful to it, and it is full of secrets to be discovered. It can change one's life. It lasts forever. Do you know why?"

"No, Miss Randolph." My voice came in a whisper.

"Because it is a language in which God speaks to anyone who will listen."

I looked at her. The plain face was transformed. Color touched her cheeks and lips and she looked quite beautiful. I was almost afraid, she looked so different.

Then she picked up my right hand and carefully placed my fingers on five keys. "Your thumb is on the note that we call middle c," she said. "That is what you must remember now. Look carefully."

I looked.

"Put your hand in your lap."

I did.

"Now place your thumb on middle c and the other fingers as I placed them for you."

I did.

"Good. Will you remember that?"

"Yes, Miss Randolph."

That day I learned how to play a scale using first one hand and then the other. After a while she said, "Now we have begun. You have learned the first commandment of music. You have begun the foundation. We will build on it."

I knew that something marvelous had happened. I felt years older than I had been when I left my house. Then Miss Randolph played for me while I sat on the green love seat.

This became our pattern. She played for me and I built on the foundation. I progressed from scales to Czerny, from Clementi to Mozart. I picked her raspberries for her, beans from her vines, grapes from her arbor. I helped her harvest her crops and she helped me plant mine for later harvesting.

One day a girl in our children's choir said, "Miss Randolph is so plain. I don't like to look at her."

I spoke before I thought. "She's beautiful. I want to be just like her."

Janyce laughed. "You probably will be."

I knew she was being unkind. Her hair was blond and curly and her wide blue eyes were fringed with thick lashes. She always looked at me as if I were an object to be swept away.

But it didn't hurt that morning because I knew I was right. Miss Randolph was teaching me a secret language that would always be mine. And she really was beautiful.

I crouched on the porch, arms about my knees, my hair falling across my face, my eyes tight shut. *If all the crows are gone from the vacant lot when I count to six, he won't die.*

In time to my heartbeats I counted from one to six and then I opened my eyes. Two crows remained on the edge of the lot. My mouth was dry, and my lips stuck together. I tried another charm.

If the smoke is still coming from Mrs. Bassett's chimney when I count to seven, he won't die.

Nails digging into my sweaty palms, toes scrunched together inside my shoes, I counted seven heartbeats. A wisp of smoke faded against the grey sky. *That counts,* I whispered. *Even if it's almost gone, it still counts. He isn't going to die.*

"Have you practiced today?" my mother asked from the doorway behind me.

"Not yet. Is he any better?"

"He's about the same." Purple shadows lay beneath my mother's eyes and she was pale. "Please bring some carrots and apples up from the cellar, will you? And then go practice."

I sighed. Usually I loved the cellar with its winter smells of apples and potatoes. I liked the orderly rows of pickles and fruits in glass jars, the vegetables in sacks of burlap, and the fragrant apples in bushel baskets. The cellar smelled of home and happiness. It made me think of meals we took together around the big old table, of apples and popcorn before the open fire, with four-year-old Martin having more fun than anyone. Now Martin, my little brother Martin, lay upstairs in his bed desperately ill and in pain.

I knew my parents had thought I was asleep when they talked one frightening night, outside Martin's room, after Dr. Barnes had left. I couldn't hear everything, but I heard the words "paralyzed" and "crippled." And I heard my mother say, in a voice so strange I hardly recognized it as hers, "I can't bear it. Not Martin. It would almost be better for him not to . . ."

"Do not say it." My father's voice was stern. "We will not give up hope."

"But to live helpless and in pain," my mother said, her voice full of tears. "Twisted and in pain forever. I can't bear it."

When I walked into the kitchen with my load of carrots and fruit, I smelled soup cooking, the tang of onions and tomatoes. Mother was slicing potatoes.

"Please put them on the cabinet. I'll wash them in a moment. Thanks, dear. Now go along and practice."

"Mother, how can you do the ordinary things when he's so sick? I can't think about anything else."

"I know," she said. "I can't, either. But your father is with him now, and we all have to eat. It's good to be busy. It really is."

I went next door to the church. The piano was in the basement Sunday school room. We didn't have a piano, so I practiced here. In summer it was pleasant and cool in this room when it was hot everywhere else, but now it was bitterly cold.

I sat down at the old upright and began my scales: up and down, hands separate, hands together. Rising and falling, one tone after the other, the scales began to take on the rhythm of words. *Do not let him die O Lord please do not let him die dear Lord.* I couldn't practice very long.

✳ ✳ ✳

At lunchtime Dr. Barnes came in to look at Martin. He sounded worried when he told my parents, "It's tonight we have to be concerned about. If he makes it through tonight, he'll have a good chance."

He ate a bowl of soup with us. "Why don't you go down and skate awhile?" he asked me. "The lake is solid and the exercise will do you good. Tim and Annie are going down. That's my prescription for you." He stood up to leave, and he put his hand on my head for a moment. "We'll do all we can, Julie. Trust me. I'll be back tonight." Then he said to my parents, "Get some rest if you can. I'll need your help tonight."

When Dr. Barnes had gone I ran upstairs to look at Martin. I had always thought he looked like one of the chubby little angels that tumbled across the ceilings of the German churches in one of Father's books. His eyes were blue, like Mother's, and his hair was a cap of yellow curls. Father said his own hair had been like that when he was a child.

Now Martin was very white and not chubby at all. I couldn't see his eyes, but I knew they wouldn't sparkle if I could see them. His yellow curls were limp and tangled. His hands twitched, and he breathed as if it hurt him, even in his sleep. I was frightened, just looking at him.

I took my skates and went down to the lake. I spotted Tim and Annie by their bright red stocking caps, and for a while I watched them skate. As far as I could see, the lake lay hard and glittering. Little shafts of light sparkled against the hummocks of ice, caught in the winter sun. Along the shore were rows of canvas tents, each one sheltering a fisherman.

I thought of the day in spring when we had come to live on the island. I had stood at the rail of the steamer watching the water and the gulls.

Father had said, "This boat is the only transportation to the island. In winter we will be island-bound."

Now, in the distance, I could see the billowing sail of the iceboat bringing mail from the mainland. I watched chunks of ice fly from the steel rudder.

Tim and Annie waved and raced up to me. But before they reached me I felt a wave of fear, fear for Martin. I turned and ran toward home, my feet slipping and sliding in the ice and snow. At home I dropped my skates on the porch and ran next door to the church. I ran down the center aisle and looked up at the window of the fishermen. I loved that window. All the men in it were real to me. They had been my friends ever since I had first seen them.

"Listen," I said, all out of breath, to the central figure in that window, the one who stood beside the little boat, talking to the fishermen. "Listen. Please don't let Martin die. I'll do whatever you say if you let him get well. You can do anything you want to me, if you just let Martin get well. Please. I promise. Amen."

The tall man continued to stretch his hands toward the nets of the fishermen. They leaned toward him as if he were going to speak. The sun made the colored glass leap and glow, but he didn't speak to any of us.

The rest of the day dragged itself out, after I went home. We ate our supper and I helped with the dishes. Finally I went to bed. I tried to stay awake but, although I heard the doctor when he came and I heard faint sounds in Martin's room, I couldn't hear what anyone said, and I couldn't make myself stay awake.

It was early when I woke up. The house was quiet. I heard creaking noises as it came awake after the night. I heard the steady ticking of the large hall clock and the scrabblings and scratchings of the mice who lived in the attic above my room. But I didn't hear any voices.

I put on my robe and slippers and walked quietly to Martin's room. The doctor was gone. Mother slept in the big armchair beside the bed, her head back, her mouth slightly open. Martin lay breathing easily, naturally. He looked like my brother again: like a little boy, not like a small old man.

After a while I went down the hall and looked inside my father's bedroom. He slept deeply.

Back in my own room I looked out the window. I saw the pear tree below in the garden, only a bunch of sticks held together by a thick trunk; the dry brown of chrysanthemum plants poking above the snow. I saw the feathery tracks of birds. And I saw the sky, grey and cloudy and cold. I was afraid to look at it very long.

All that day I waited. I watched my parents smile at each other and at me. Over and over again I peeked in at Martin, still sleeping. And I waited.

Dr. Barnes looked tired when he came at noon, but he was happy when he came down into the kitchen from Martin's room. "I told you we'd do it," he said to me. "He'll be gathering the first wildflowers with you this spring."

Still I couldn't speak.

When he told us good-bye he said, "There's another child sick on one of the other islands. They say the ice is thick enough, so I'm driving over, but I'll look in again tomorrow. Remember, keep his room moist and warm."

But he didn't come back the next day. My mother answered our phone and her voice was full of horror when she said, "Oh Mrs. Barnes, how terrible! Yes, I'll tell my husband right away."

She turned to my father and said, "The doctor's car went through the ice. He was trapped in it."

"*Ach, du lieber Gott!*" My father put on his wraps and hurried out to be with Mrs. Barnes and Tim and Annie.

I thought of the cold, dark waters of the lake, and Dr. Barnes down there. Were his eyes open? Did he know he was going to die? I went to the church and walked toward the window of the fishermen. "Why did you do it?" I asked the one to whom I had made my promise. "It isn't fair. You were supposed to do it to me."

✳ ✳ ✳

Each day Martin became a little stronger. Each day I was happy for a while. Then I would think of Dr. Barnes and I would be overwhelmed with guilt and fear. A huge, threatening darkness hung over me.

One morning Father said to me, "Come. You are pale. Let us go for a walk, you and I." So we put on our sweaters. Outside he said, "I can smell spring coming. *Der Frühling, der Frühling*," he sang. "Can you smell it, *liebchen?*"

Before I could answer him I began to cry. He held me for a long time and finally, between gulping sobs that came from deep inside me, I told him all about the promise I had made.

"I said he could do anything to me if he'd make Martin well," I told him. "He was supposed to do it to me. Not to Dr. Barnes. To me. It's my fault that Dr. Barnes died. And maybe something will still happen to me. Something terrible. I promised."

"Look at me." My father cupped my chin in his big hand and tilted my head so that I looked right into his eyes. "Dr. Barnes's death is not your fault. It is a tragic accident. It is not your fault, not anybody's fault. He is a hero. A quiet hero, but a hero nonetheless. He has given his life for a friend."

While he spoke, he wiped my face with his big white handkerchief. Then he took my hand and we went into the church together. We sat in one of the pews, and my father's arm was around my shoulder. We just sat there together, looking at the window of the fishermen.

Finally Father said, "Look at his hands."

I looked. Then I noticed that all the men were looking at his hands. Those hands were held with both palms up, the strong fingers spread out.

I looked down at my own hands as they lay in my lap, and I moved my fingers. If you take something, I thought, your fingers curl up. If you give something, your fingers reach out.

That was the thing I had missed. He wasn't taking; he was giving. And on the day I made my promise he'd been giving. Not taking. Giving. I took a deep breath. I was surprised to find tears on my cheeks again, because I wasn't afraid anymore.

Father and I sat there awhile watching sunlight pour through the window, watching color break into rainbows all around us.

CHAPTER
ELEVEN

———— 🍇 ————

Summer days on the island lay ahead of me full of promise, full of freedom and imagined delights. There seemed no end to the possibilities for pleasure. I rode my bike and swam in the lake. Raspberries waited to be gathered, and peaches. There were picnics with Martin, and music and reading.

I especially treasured the walks along the lake and through the woods to visit my special friend, Mr. Norton. He was old and wise. He leaned on a cane when he walked, and his hands trembled. But his eyes crinkled around the corners, and I knew there was nothing that did not interest him. We talked about important things, and he never laughed at anything I said. He always answered my questions seriously and after consideration.

We discussed, for example, the moon. "In your lifetime," Mr. Norton calmly predicted, "people will go there. People will walk on the surface of the moon and bring us back the truth about it."

"But how?" I asked. "How will they get there and back again?"

"There will be ways."

Of course we talked about God. "What do you think God's really like?" I asked.

"I'll tell you," Mr. Norton answered, "what I think God is *not* like. I think God is not an old man with a long beard. I think God is not only up there—" He pointed to the sky. "And I think God does not necessarily exist just to be asked or thanked for favors."

This was not too strange for me to manage because I knew that my parents had thoughts very much like these. But it was comforting to discuss such matters with someone else as well.

"Did you ever consider," Mr. Norton spoke in a slow, dreamy way, "that God might be rather like a thought— like the secret voice each of us has inside? You know. The secret voice. The one each of us has that is like no other?"

I pondered that for a while. "But what about me?" I wanted to know. "What does God think about me?"

Mr. Norton paused quite a long time before he spoke. "God might think that you must listen to that voice that is inside you," he said finally. "That you must listen to all the voices of Nature. You must hear all the voices; the beautiful and the ugly. And then you must answer them, after you have listened. That is what you must do with your life."

I had hoped, now that I was almost ten, I could really begin to understand these things. I hoped that the summer would stretch out long and calm so that I could be with Mr. Norton often. I kept thinking of new questions to ask him.

One morning I had gathered dandelions and clover as I walked to his house, and I sat on a tree stump for a while, braiding a chain of them to wear. The blossoms smelled of summer, and my fingers were stained and sticky with their juices.

Mr. Norton was sitting on the porch, and he waved to me as soon as he saw me. When I came closer he greeted me. "That is a splendid necklace. Better than riches or fine raiment. More precious than rubies or diamonds." I loved the way he talked. "Do you know how dandelions perpetuate themselves?"

I was not even sure what the question meant, so I just said no.

"By a dance in the wind," he said. "By listening to Nature. Nature always has something to say. Rain talks, and lightning. Water and trees. Clouds and birds. And thunder. Oh yes, thunder surely talks. Listen all the time." He looked at me steadily, the way he always did. But I thought there was something new in his look. "Watch and listen, but don't be afraid. Even when the voice seems loud and terrible there is always a reason. And there may be something good on the other side of the voice, even when it is most frightening."

I didn't stay long that morning. I thought he looked different somehow. Tired. Older. I gave him my dandelion necklace, and he was holding it, touching and smelling it when I left him.

That night there was a storm. I didn't like electrical storms. But this time I didn't go into my mother's room, or my father's, for comfort as I usually did when I woke, frightened. Mr. Norton had told me to listen, so I listened.

I heard the steady rush of rain. I heard the wind roaring like an angry ghost. The lightning was so bright that it seemed as if I heard it, too. And the thunder. Oh, the thunder. And then, among all the other sounds came a sound so terrible that I did not know how to listen to it. But I recognized it. It was the death sound of a tree. I listened as it groaned and strained, and finally, as it fell.

My mother came to me then, and sat on my bed. "Don't be afraid," she said quietly. "Did you hear the tree fall?"

"Yes," I told her. "I heard it all."

"It was a very old tree," my mother said, "and its roots had weakened over the years." She bent to kiss me. "Go back to sleep. The storm is nearly over."

As I lay there growing sleepy again, the wind began to die down and the thunder became more distant. I thought of Mr. Norton. *I listened*, I told him silently. *I listened*. And just before I slept I heard, inside my mind, his secret voice saying my name.

CHAPTER
T W E L V E

———————— 🍇 ————————

I had thought my father was perfect. I trusted him the way one trusts water to drink or air to breathe. Without question. And then he began to change. I did not understand it. A shadow seemed to follow him, and I began to walk carefully through the days of my life.

It was on a Good Friday morning the year I was ten that I was caught in a storm that raged over Eden. All during Lent I thought my father seemed sad. He didn't want to read to Martin and me. At mealtimes he hardly talked at all. I knew that Lent was a time when we were supposed to think less about ourselves and more about preparing for Easter. But I didn't understand why that could make my father spend most of his time in the study, or why it made him quiet and stern.

"What's the matter with Father?" I asked my mother more than once during that long season.

"I'm not sure," she would answer me, looking sad. Or, "He is unhappy just now. We must be patient."

That Good Friday morning my mother said, "Don't go into your father's study this morning. He's busy preparing for the three-hour service and he doesn't want to be disturbed."

I didn't mean to disturb him. It was just that I found his silver pocket knife under the big chair in the living room. We had all been looking for it for days. My jack ball rolled under the chair. I reached for it, and there was the knife.

I thought Father would be delighted. I hurried to the study and went in without knocking. "Father," I called, "look. I found your pocket knife. It was under the big chair. See." I took it to him.

He looked at me. He did not even notice the knife. "Were you not told to stay out of this room today?"

He had never spoken to me like that before, and it was hard to answer because I could hardly speak.

"Were you not told?" His voice was like a stranger's. "Answer me."

"Yes, Father."

"Then leave me. At once."

It seemed to take me a long time to walk to the kitchen where Mother was finishing the breakfast dishes. Martin was coloring in his favorite spot under the kitchen table. He didn't look up when I came in. He was coloring a lamb, and it was black.

Mother looked at me. "What's the matter? Are you sick?" She put her cool hand on my forehead. "You don't have a fever. Is something wrong?"

I wondered if I'd ever be happy again. "I made Father angry," I said.

She asked quickly, "What did you do?"

"I went into his study. I thought he'd be glad. I found his pocket knife." I held it toward her. "He wasn't glad. He was angry."

Mother looked troubled. "I told you not to bother him this morning. Remember?"

I nodded. Tears began to slide down my face and I licked them off. They tasted salty and bitter. "Will he always be angry with me?"

"Of course not," she said. "I'm sorry. But I warned you. This is an especially hard time for your father and we must help him all we can." She hesitated. Then she said, "There are things about your father that are not easy to understand. You remember that I told you about his first wife, Elsa?" My mother's eyes were troubled.

"The one who died? With her little baby?"

"Yes." Mother knelt in front of me, and we looked at each other. "It was at this time of year, the spring, that they died. The memory makes him very sad." She held me, and I felt my tears start again. When she drew back I saw that tears stood in her eyes, too.

"Please don't cry," I said. "I'm the one who was bad."

"You weren't bad. You were thoughtless. There's a difference. It will be all right. You'll see." She kissed me. "But we must all try not to make him angry."

Martin, from his secret place under the table, said, "I don't like him." He sounded as if he were thinking about something else, and he went on coloring his black lamb.

Mother sighed. "You don't mean that, honey. Come on now. We'll get ready for church."

In church my father stood before us, solemn and distant in his black cassock. Although he looked at me, he did not seem to know me. He had told me that Good Friday was the darkest day of all the year, and I thought this one would surely go on forever.

During that service quite suddenly I felt that the Psalms had been written especially for me. When we read, "Thy wrathful displeasure goeth over me, and the fear of thee hath undone me," I wasn't sure whether I was talking to God or to my father.

Of course the day ended, the sun shone, and Easter came after all. But shadows remained around me, menacing.

CHAPTER
THIRTEEN

---❦---

I liked the basement Sunday school room. It smelled of chalk, old books, and the tangy scent that my Sunday school teacher used.

Mrs. Moffat.

She seemed very old. Her hair was interesting because we never knew what color it might be on a given Sunday morning. Often it was variegated. Once it was definitely green, and Mrs. Moffat appeared to be upset all morning.

She was proud. She wore the tweedy clothes of the Lady of the Manor, for she was British: emphatically, aristocratically British. How she came to be on our island I didn't know. I didn't think about it. She was there and I was glad. She was, my father said, Church of England, and the things she taught us resounded in the King's English. They still do, in my inner ear.

Mrs. Moffat taught us our catechism, and she was thorough. Over and over she questioned and we answered.

Question: "What is thy duty towards thy neighbor?"

Answer: "My duty towards my neighbor is to love him as myself, and to do to all men as I would they should do unto me."

Mrs. Moffat had explained to us that "him" and "men" meant all of us. Not just the boys. The girls, too. And Mrs. Moffat added a question of her own: Who is my neighbor?

Answer: A human being, like myself, who needs my help.

It was so simple. On the island, I thought, we were all neighbors. We helped each other. When we were land-locked in winter, when anyone was sick, we helped each other. There were no questions, only action.

But one day after choir practice Janyce said to me, "My mother says that I can't play with anyone who is friends with Ada Lincoln. My father says that her parents are sinners and that makes the whole family sinful and I am not to associate with any of them. You'd better be careful."

I had no idea what she meant. Ada Lincoln had become my best friend. She was my age, and we did everything together. We were in the same class at school. We got our bikes at the same time and we rode all over the island together. We constructed elaborate fantasies of ways in which we could always be friends, ways to insure that we would never be parted. It was as though we unconsciously suspected the possibility of separation.

Ada's sister was Lily and her younger brother was Ken. Mrs. Lincoln was a quiet woman, gentle and welcoming. After school she would give us bread and butter and brown sugar. We were allowed to eat any of the golden pears that fell from the old tree out in back, but we were forbidden to pick the fruit from the tree. I was always a bit uneasy when Ken would shake the tree violently so that the pears would fall and we could eat them without really having broken a commandment.

I had often admired Ada's skin, and Lily's too. Mine was so pale and freckled. Theirs was the color of coffee with cream in it. Mrs. Lincoln's was white, like my mother's. But Mr. Lincoln was different. His skin was dark, dark brown, almost black. He worked on one of the steamers that sailed between our island and the mainland. On the rare occasions when he was at home, he treated me gravely, as if I were already grown up.

Once, when our parents and Martin and I were crossing to the mainland, I saw Mr. Lincoln on the boat. He was tall and dignified in his white coat. Although he saw us, he did not speak to any of us, but he nodded.

Then I heard a man call to him, "Hey boy, step on it. I don't want to wait all day for that drink."

Mr. Lincoln answered softly, "Yes sir, right away."

I turned to my father, not understanding. He said, "We'll talk about this later." I knew that meant *Don't ask me anything now.*

But that evening when we were home again Mother asked, "Have you noticed anything different about Mr. Lincoln?"

"Different?" I was puzzled.

"Yes." My mother's eyes searched my face.

"I know," Martin said.

"Tell us," Mother smiled at him.

"Well," he said thoughtfully, "Mr. Lincoln is chocolate and we are vanilla."

Oh, that, I thought. Mother nodded gravely. We were careful not to laugh at Martin because if we did, he withdrew from us. "That's a good way to put it, honey," she said. "Mr. Lincoln is a black man. His skin is different from ours because we are white people."

I said, "Mrs. Lincoln is white, like us, isn't she?"

"Yes," Mother said. "And the children are a mixture. They are not as dark as their father and not as light as their mother."

"Janyce says she can't play with them because her parents say they are sinners. And she won't be my friend, either, if I'm Ada's friend. Why?"

Mother's lips set, for a moment, in that grim line they had when she was angry or upset.

Father, who had been listening to us finally spoke. "Janyce and her parents are wrong. It is true that many people are offended when there is a mixed marriage, a marriage between black and white. But this marriage is sanctified, as are all marriages performed in the Church. Their life is hard. Hard. And we must do what we can to make it easier. Do you not think so?"

"So I can still be friends with Ada?"

"Of course," Mother said.

"Good. I don't care if I can't be friends with Janyce. She doesn't like me and I don't like her, either."

My parents looked at each other, but before they could speak I said, "I don't think Lily has a best friend." I thought about her, always alone, always remote and quiet.

"It is sad." My father sounded sad himself.

"I could be Ken's friend if I were older," Martin said. "If he'd let me."

"I'm sure you would, honey." Mother hugged him.

"The one place where that family should feel absolutely safe is in the Church," my father said. "I will talk with Janyce and her parents. I hope they will listen."

And the next Sunday, sitting beside Ada in our Sunday school class, when Mrs. Moffat asked us, "What is thy duty toward thy neighbor?" this time I thought to myself, *To love her*, and I was happy inside because I knew it was true.

CHAPTER
FOURTEEN

━━━━━━━━━━ ❦ ━━━━━━━━━━

And it was summer—warm, beautiful summer. I had finished reading "The Snow Queen." I sighed and closed the book, wishing the story could go on and on.

I could hear Father out on the porch, singing to Martin in his deep, rumbling voice. It was a song about a little boy and his pony. Martin loved that song from the time he was a baby.

It was a good omen, I thought, that Father sang and Martin laughed. I hoped these warm feelings would last, that we, like Gerda and Kay, might live happily ever after.

That was the summer I met Marian Foster, our last summer on the island. And it was at that time I had an accident. I was walking barefoot in my mother's sewing room one morning, and I stepped on a needle. Only part of it came away in my hand when I tried to pull it out.

Going to my mother I said, "I stepped on a needle just now, and I can't find all of it." I showed her the piece of the needle I had pulled from the sole of my foot.

She looked worried. "Does it hurt?"

"Not anymore." We looked for the rest of the needle. We did not find it. Since my foot no longer hurt, my mother said that the rest of the needle was probably on the floor somewhere and it would be swept up. I tried to forget about it, thinking that perhaps adults had a certain magic that could make a bad thing disappear if it were ignored long enough.

Since I knew we would be leaving the island at the end of the summer, I spent all the time I could outdoors memorizing the things I loved, the things I'd have to leave. I walked by the lake and through the woods. I wanted snow in midsummer so I could see the cedar boughs covered with white, still and sparkling. I went into the German bakery, but the smells weren't right, for the fragrances I liked best came at Christmastime when Mrs. Klein baked *springerlie* and *lebkuchen*.

Mrs. Klein sensed my sadness. "*Liebchen*," she said one morning when I went in, "you will come back and visit us one day. It will not be good-bye for always. Here. Have a tart."

She handed me a raspberry tart, and I tried to smile at her. I wasn't hungry, but I took it and walked along the road that led to the old Anderson place. In all the time we had been on the island, no one had lived there. It was an old mansion set far back off the road. Trees intertwined their branches, like the ones in the story of Philemon and Baucis. Hydrangea bushes grew tall and rank, the blossoms heavy and strangely colored, like Easter eggs that didn't quite take the dye. Rose bushes sent up gangly sucker branches among the neglected blooms. Sweet Williams and pinks were profuse and spicy.

On this particular morning, walking along the path to the house, trying to ignore the sharp stabs in my foot, I thought I heard music. I was sure of it as I came closer. I heard a piano and a woman's voice weaving in and out of the sounds it made. I stopped to listen, and when the music was finished I went up on the porch and stood looking into the room through the screen door.

Two people were in that room: a young woman and an older man. The man was seated at the keyboard of a big, shiny black piano. It was quite different from the upright on which I practiced. The girl stood behind him, looking over his shoulder at the music on the rack.

As I watched them she said, "Once more please, Father. I can do better than that."

The man turned to look up at her and he said, "Rest awhile, Marian. We'll come back to it." Then he stood up and stretched. As he turned, he saw me standing there on the porch and he came to open the door.

"Marian, we have a guest." He motioned for me to come in.

"I'm sorry," I stammered. "I didn't know anyone lived here. I walk here sometimes." I was embarrassed at having eavesdropped. My mother would be ashamed of me.

"Please do come in." The girl spoke to me. Her voice, when she spoke, was as beautiful as it had been when she sang. I wanted to listen to the sound of it. I had never heard such a beautiful voice. She was tall, and I thought she must be quite old. Sixteen, perhaps. She wore a dress the color of butter. Her thick, dark hair was caught at the nape of her neck with a large yellow bow. Her eyes were dark, too, with long lashes. Although she smiled at me, I thought she did not look really happy.

I went in. Marian's father stood beside her. He was tall, also, with thick, silver hair that curled above his collar. He was elegant. I was sure of that. *Elegant* was a word my father used in describing certain things. Our old silver pitcher was elegant, and the small bisque statue that stood on the table my mother's grandfather had made. I knew that these were two elegant people, like the people in a book.

"Our name is Foster," the man told me. "I am David Foster, and this is my daughter, Marian."

"How do you do?" I shook hands with both of them, and I told them my name. "I live on the island, too. But we have to leave it at the end of the summer."

"How sad that must make you." Mr. Foster spoke to me as if he, a stranger, knew how much I loved the island. I was ashamed of my dusty shoes and my rumpled skirt and blouse, and of my hands, sticky from the tart I had eaten.

"Please stay and have tea with us. We were just stopping for a while," Mr. Foster said. "Then after tea perhaps Marian will sing for us."

Marian went into another room, and I heard dishes touching each other and the sound of water running. "I hope she will sing," I told Mr. Foster.

"Do you like music?"

"Oh yes. More than anything, almost. I study piano with Miss Randolph."

"What are you working on now?"

"A Clementi sonatina," I told him.

"Good. Good." He nodded. "Clementi is an appetizer for Mozart." As Marian came in with a tray, he stood to take it from her. "How nice it looks." He smiled at her. "And how good it smells."

I watched Marian's hands move among the china and silver tea things. Everything she did was graceful. I liked the way she and her father acted together. As if they were best friends.

When we had finished our tea Mr. Foster said, "Marian, do you feel like singing for us?"

"All right," she said, and she walked toward the piano. It seemed to me that she didn't really want to sing. She spent quite a long time looking through the pieces of music, turning pages. She finally began to sing, but I soon realized that something was wrong. She was having trouble breathing. She began to gasp, and each breath was labored and frightening.

Mr. Foster left the room quickly and returned with a hypodermic needle. He filled it from a small bottle. "Just a moment now," he said to Marian. "It will soon be easier." He rubbed a place on her arm with damp cotton and then he gave her an injection.

Quite soon her breathing eased. "I'm sorry to behave like this on your first visit," Marian said, looking at me. Her voice was weak and hoarse and it made me sad to hear it.

Before I could answer, Mr. Foster said, "I'm sorry, too, Marian. That was a bad one, wasn't it?" He was calm, as if this had happened before. He turned to me. "Marian has asthma, and we are not certain what causes it. She has been much better recently. Since we have come to the island."

I was still frightened. "I think I'd better go," I said. "My mother will be wondering about me. Thank you very much for the tea. I hope you'll be better again soon, Marian."

"Perhaps Marian will sing for you the next time you visit us," Mr. Foster said. "Do come again, won't you? It is good to have friends in a strange place."

At home, I told my parents about the Fosters.

"Yes, we have met them," Father said.

I was surprised. "Why didn't you tell me? They have a grand piano. Marian has the most beautiful voice. I heard her sing. But sometimes she can't breathe. Her father told me what it is, but I can't remember."

My parents looked at each other. "It is called asthma," Father explained.

"Yes, that's it. She'll get better, won't she? Her father said she has been better lately."

My father pulled at his pipe. His face was troubled and his speech, as always when he was sad or worried, took on its German inflection. "Yes, we hope she will be completely well soon." He looked at me for quite a long time. Then he said, "She is under the shadow of a great cruelty that she suffered last winter."

"No, Karl." My mother's tone was sharp. "No. She's too young. Don't tell her."

"I do not intend to tell her any more," Father said. "It is a confidence, in any case. But we know already that people can be cruel to each other. Dr. Hendrick has told me the girl's story only because he thought I might be able to help in some way."

I hoped he could help. I hoped someone could help.

Martin wanted to go with me the next time I walked to the Anderson place, but I wouldn't let him. I wanted it to belong to me. My foot didn't hurt quite as much, or else I was getting used to it. Marian was there alone, singing. She stopped when I came up on the porch.

"Come in, Julie." She unhooked the screen door.

"Please don't stop singing," I begged her. "Can I listen?"

"I'm just doing exercises," she said, "but you may listen if you want to. Father has gone to the village and I'm glad to have company."

I listened as she sang scales and leaps, slow and rapid passages. I thought her voice was like a goldfish darting in and out of its castle in a glass bowl. When she had stopped I said, "Oh Marian, I love to hear you sing. You won't have asthma now, will you, just because you sang?"

She frowned. "No, of course not." Then, as if she wanted to talk about something else, she asked, "Would you like to see my room?"

The room was exactly right for her. Everything was perfect. I couldn't stop looking at the picture that hung on one wall. It was a painting of a lion. He was golden and proud and he stood in long grass, just staring out past us.

Marian saw me looking at it. "You like my lion? I sometimes try to imagine the country where he lives. He is free and brave. He can do just as he likes. No matter what happened to him, he would always be like that."

All at once Marian's voice sounded fierce. "I hate the world," she said. "I want to stay here on the island forever and never go back to the world again."

"But Marian, the island is part of the world," I said.

"You don't know anything about it." She sounded angry with me. "You are too young. You don't know anything. You don't understand anything."

I shivered deep inside. I wanted to comfort her, but she was right. I didn't know anything. I only knew she had been hurt somehow and I couldn't do anything about it. I had felt safe. As long as I was with my family, I had thought, nothing bad could touch me from outside. But Marian had been with her father, and he hadn't been able to protect her from whatever it was. Sometimes I thought I never wanted to grow up. I wanted to stay here, safe and happy on the island forever, with my father the way he used to be.

That night I asked him, "Please, Father, can't you tell me what it was that happened to Marian?"

"No, I have told you. It is her secret. I do not have the right."

"She told me partly. She said she hates the world."

"Yes, I can understand. Poor Marian. There are terrible ways in which people can hurt each other. It is a sadness of life, that cruelty, and Marian is a victim. We must hope that the peace of this island will help her recover. She is young, and her father is wise. We must hope that soon she will find a way, her own way, to be strong and whole."

"Like her lion," I said, and I told my father about the painting.

"Yes," he said, "a lion is a fine animal. A king among animals. But she needs a lion inside her, I think, and not only on her wall. We all need a lion inside."

Soon after that my parents and I went to have dinner with the Fosters. The room was beautiful by candlelight. A lamp with a stained-glass shade hung above the piano and the rug repeated its reds and blues. I liked the parchment with ancient musical instruments, like the one I had seen in a book.

Marian served us a soufflé and fresh asparagus. My father was pleased with a light golden wine. "Like the Rhine," he said as he held it to the light and watched small bubbles rise and break in the crystal goblet. And for dessert we had red raspberries, freshly picked, and cream.

After dinner Mr. Foster asked Marian to sing. "We are friends here," he told her. "All friends."

I did not know the names of the songs she sang that night as her father played, but I wanted her to sing on and on.

When she had finished my father said softly, "What a wonderful gift. I think you will become one of the great singers. A true artist. And we will remember that we heard you here, tonight, when you were young."

Marian started to speak. But suddenly she put her hand against her chest and I saw her struggle. I heard the painful, rasping breaths. Her father led her from the room, his arm around her.

When he came back he said, "Marian sends you her good-night wishes. She is going to rest now."

"*Ja*," my father said, "she needs to rest. But one day her body will be strong enough to contain her art. That will be a splendid day, when she is whole."

We left then, and while we were walking home my foot began to hurt so much that I couldn't stand it any more. I felt as if I were walking on the blade of a knife. I knew that each painful step was taking me away from the island to a world where there were dangers I didn't understand. I began to cry.

"*Liebchen*, what is it?" Father's tone was concerned.

"It's my needle," I told him. "And I don't want to leave the island, and I'm afraid for Marian. Maybe she won't ever get well. Maybe she won't ever be a singer. And . . ."

The whole story came out then: the accident with the needle, my fears for Marian, my fears for myself. My father picked me up and carried me the rest of the way home.

My mother cried. "I'll never forgive myself. Never."

"Then we will have to help you," my father said. His voice was kind, the way it always used to be.

"Oh yes," I said, reaching to touch Mother. "It wasn't your fault."

"It was. It was my fault," she insisted.

"It is important to forgive oneself," Father said. "But it is a hard lesson to learn. Even harder than it is to learn to forgive another."

In the morning my father took me to see Dr. Hendrick. We told him about the needle. He used the X-ray machine and in a little while he showed me the picture. I saw a thin, small, sliver of steel there near a bone in my foot. It was strange to think that it was a part of me.

"When there is something inside that is harming one, it has to come out," the doctor told me, "or it can cause serious trouble. Sometimes we have to bear a small pain in order to prevent a larger one. I'll try very hard not to hurt you."

He did, though. He hurt me when he gave me an injection before he started and again when he took the stitches. And later that afternoon, lying in my bed in a darkened room, I felt the pain in my foot coming in pulses like a giant, evil heartbeat.

Just as the pain pills were starting to work, Marian came in to see me. She sat by my bed looking fresh and cool and smelling of violets.

"I'm so sorry," she said.

"Please sing to me."

"If you want me to." But she was silent for a long moment. Then she asked, "Julie, how long has the needle been in your foot? How long has it been hurting you?"

"Almost all summer," I told her, "but not all the time. I knew it was there. I wanted it to go away so much that I pretended it wasn't there. So did my mother."

I was growing drowsy and the pain was riding away from me on little waves. "Dr. Hendrick says sometimes we have to cut a thing out so it won't cause trouble. Maybe he could take away the thing that caused your asthma."

My voice went on its own way and it seemed to me that someone else was speaking, not myself. "I hope you are going to be all right. Don't be afraid, Marian. But I'm afraid, too, so I guess I can't tell you not to be. I'm afraid to leave the island and go out there in the other world."

I didn't hear her speak, but just before I went to sleep she began to sing and I heard her voice, silvery and sweet, floating in and out of the shadows in my room.

Later, when I woke, my foot still hurt, but not as sharply as it had. I caught a faint scent of violets, and I remembered Marian. Then I saw it. Propped up on my dresser, looking toward me, was Marian's lion. I must have cried out because my mother hurried into the room.

"What is it, dear? Does it hurt?"

"Not very much. I was just surprised to see Marian's lion."

Mother sat on my bed and took my hand. "She brought it while you were sleeping. She put it there so you'd see it when you woke up. She said you'd understand."

Then my father came into the room. "Are you feeling better?"

"Yes. But Father, Marian gave me her lion. She shouldn't give it away. She needs it."

"You must trust her," my father said. "Perhaps things are changing for her. Do you think this might be true?"

I knew then that Marian didn't need her lion anymore. He was mine now. She had brought him to go with me on my journey to the world outside.

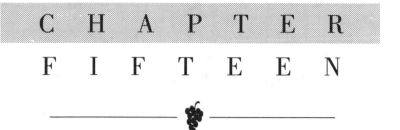

CHAPTER
FIFTEEN

I moved through the final days of that last island summer feeling as if I were two people. Half of me moved in sunlight, half in shadow. When my father was kind, when he smiled, the bright side of myself spread until it nearly covered the shadowy side. But when he became angry and spoke to me in his cold voice, I walked in the dark.

Once, after an especially bad morning, I went out to the back yard where Mother and Martin sat on the grass playing with a striped red and yellow ball.

Mother looked at me. "Are you all right?"

"I guess so." I sat beside them. "What makes Father get so angry? I don't like it when he does. He's different."

She pulled a few blades of grass and I watched her twist them between her fingers as she talked. "He has terrible headaches and they make him tense," she said. "He has many things on his mind, too. Bishop DuVal's visit, our move to South Dakota. He doesn't mean to be cross. I know he doesn't."

"It scares me."

"I know."

Martin went over to swing in the old tire that hung by a thick rope from a branch of the elm tree. He lay on his stomach, his head turned toward us, his feet out behind. He was thin, since his illness, and had lost that happy look he used to have. Even his curly hair didn't have its usual bounce. He looked past us. It was hard to tell what he was thinking.

Mother said, "You're old enough to know . . ."

A shaft of sunlight crossed her skirt, turning the creamy cloth to gold. I asked, "Old enough to know what?"

"I mean that you are old enough to try to understand that sometimes people can't help the way they act. Your father doesn't mean to be the way he is sometimes. He just can't help it."

The sun went behind a cloud, and I felt a sudden chill. But I didn't know what to say.

Mother went on. "Bishop DuVal is coming on the afternoon boat. He'll be here for dinner and he'll spend the night."

I loved the old bishop. He had brought me a copy of Greek myths the last time he came. It had the most beautiful pictures in it. And he brought Martin a book about a white pony.

The bishop's eyes were friendly when he looked at Martin and me. He would take Martin on his lap and then we would watch while the bishop performed magic.

"*Enfin, mes enfants,*" he would say, "watch carefully." He would show us a coin on the palm of his hand. Then he'd close his hand and when he opened it again the coin was gone. He'd search for it and then, in great surprise, he'd take it from Martin's ear. I loved the look on Martin's face when that happened.

Often he spoke to us in French, his own language, and he had taught me some French words.

"May I go down to meet him?" I asked my mother.

"You'd better ask your father about that."

Father would not let me go down to meet the boat that afternoon. He said he and the bishop had many things to discuss and that I was not to disturb them. "You will have your chance to talk with him later," Father said.

When I saw Father and the bishop coming up our walk, I ran to meet them. *"Bonjour, Monsieur,"* I called.

The bishop smiled at me. But Father didn't smile. He used that voice that frightened me. "I told you that you were not to disturb us. You are disobedient. Go to your room."

For a moment I couldn't move.

"At once." That voice came to me through a heavy cloud.

I went to my room. Alone and desolate I thought, *Now the bishop will know how bad I am. Maybe he won't like me any more, or want me for a friend.*

When Mother finally called me I went down to set the table for dinner. I could feel her nervousness. It was a strange meal. Martin wouldn't talk at all.

"Martin," the bishop said, "do you know what I liked best of all to eat when I was a boy, like you?"

Martin only looked at his plate. He wouldn't speak. Not even when Father said, in his stern voice, the one I didn't like, "Martin, the bishop asked you a question."

"It is not important, my friend," the bishop said to Father. "Days present themselves when one does not feel like talking. *N'est-ce pas?*"

When he complimented my mother on her cooking, she thanked him. But I knew they were only pretending to talk to each other. The important things they wanted to say were hidden.

After the meal Bishop DuVal went with Father to the study and I helped Mother with the dishes. Martin sat under the table talking to his imaginary friend, Alexander. I heard him say, ". . . and then the prince chopped off the monster's head and they lived happily ever after."

I was surprised when the bishop came into the kitchen later. He came to me and took my hand. He asked my mother, "May my young friend and I walk for a while before it is time for her to go to bed?"

"Yes, of course," she said.

He asked me, "Will you please take me to one of your favorite spots?"

We went toward the cemetery. He walked with his hands clasped behind him, and he didn't talk, but when we reached the graveyard he looked around for a moment. Then he said, "Ah, yes."

Grass had grown around the gravestones. Dandelions and wild sweet grass grew at random, and clover and spicy pinks. I took the bishop's hand and led him to my favorite statue, and we just stood and looked at it for a while.

It was the white marble statue of a little girl. She was about my size, and she looked out across the graveyard toward the village. Behind her, one hand outstretched, great wings enfolding her like a cloak, was an angel. I knew them both: the child and the angel. I talked to them often. I had named the stone child with my own name.

The bishop asked, "Do you come here often?"

"Sometimes. Mostly when I want to think about things. Or when I'm sad."

"And is that often?"

It was hard to talk over the big lump that was forming in my throat. I looked away.

The bishop said, "Come. Let us sit down here."

We sat on a smooth marble slab that had fallen long ago. It lay like a white bridge over the grass.

"*Tiens*. What is it that makes you so sad?" His voice was kind and I felt he would understand anything I told him. I knew that he still liked me, after all.

"My father makes me sad," I began. "He gets so angry with me. And with my mother and Martin. With everybody. And there's something else I can't understand at all."

"Try to tell me, *chérie*."

When I looked into the bishop's eyes I knew I had to tell him the truth. He would know if I didn't. "I don't understand how my father can love me, when he treats me as if he doesn't." I fought to keep from crying. I talked into those eyes that looked at me lovingly. "Sometimes he loves us and sometimes he doesn't. Sometimes he helps people and sometimes he yells at them."

My words raced, tripping over each other, pouring out in a flood. "I don't understand how can he be a minister who's supposed to be good and kind, and then act so different. I don't understand it at all. Why doesn't God stop him?"

My face grew warm. I thought I would burst with my swelling anger and misery. I looked up at the stone child and saw her, protected by the wing of the angel. I wished that I could trade places with her. I told the bishop so.

Then he did a strange thing. He leaned toward me and I felt his long, slender finger trace the sign of a cross on my forehead. His eyes closed, and his lips formed some words, but I could not tell what they were.

"My dear Julie. My dear, dear child. Listen to me now, carefully, and try to remember what I say to you."

I knew I would never forget what he said.

"Your father is a man in pain. He is, quite literally, beside himself, for he is not whole. He is divided within himself. His life has been so tragic, so difficult." He paused for a moment and then he asked me, "Do you know what I am saying?"

"I think so. You mean the wife who died and their baby? And the time he had to leave the college because of the war. When I was small. Before Martin was even born. Those things?"

"Yes. Those things. You must try to understand that when your father seems to be angry with his family he is really more angry with himself. He loves you deeply, you and Martin and your mother. He becomes angry and unkind not because he doesn't love you, but because he is suffering. So what must you try to do, in this case?"

I thought of the way Father acted when he wasn't angry. The way he sang to Martin and read to me. The way he helped Mother when she needed it. I whispered, "Try to forgive him?"

The bishop touched my cheek. "Yes, *chérie*. Try hard, for both your sakes. You are very young, but I believe you can understand. Your father has tried to forgive those who were cruel to him. I know he has. Still, he cannot. And when we cannot forgive, we suffer. Do you know?"

I thought about that. "You mean like the times when Martin and I fight about something and I stay mad? I feel bad until after we've made up?"

"Exactly." The bishop sounded pleased. "Your father will not feel really well, really happy, until he has at last been able to forgive those who wronged him. And it is a hard thing to do. A hard thing.

"Now there is another thing we must talk about, *ma petite*. Something even more difficult to comprehend. Why, you have asked me, does God not stop your father when he is not being a good priest?

"God gives each of us a choice, *chérie*. Whatever we choose, he will not stop us. That is why it is so important to choose well. In large things and small. Let me ask you something. What has your father told you about being a priest? Has he talked to you about it? About what it means to him?"

"He's told me that he is always my father, but that when he wears his stole he's God's servant first."

"*Bien*. Good. Yes, that is true. Now here is a strange truth. When a man is a good priest and serves God well, that is an excellent thing. But when a man becomes a priest and promises to serve God well and fails, for one reason or another, that is sad. But he is still God's servant, nevertheless, and what he does in God's service is good. Even when he, the man, is not. It is a great mystery. I will say it in very grown-up words because you, my little friend, have a grown-up heart. The Word does not change with the speaker."

I believed all he said. I believed it, even though I could not understand all of it. I looked at the stone child, sheltered by the stone angel. The bishop looked, too. Then he said, "You have your own angel who never leaves you. Did you know that? It is another mystery, and it is true. You have an angel who walks with you always."

He rose and took my hand and we stood together in front of my statue. My hand was warm in the bishop's big warm hand, and when I touched the child she felt warm, too. I knew I'd never see her again. But it was all right.

Fireflies sprinkled bits of light around us as the bishop and I walked out of the graveyard, through the summer twilight, toward home.

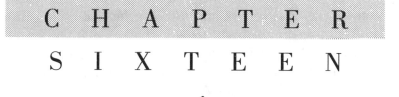

CHAPTER

SIXTEEN

A t the end of the summer we left the island and moved to a small town in South Dakota. I was lost and lonely. I thought South Dakota was ugly. I longed for the lake, the woods, the vineyards.

I hated this little town. The uninteresting buildings on Main Street all looked alike. The brick paving hurt my feet, and the few trees looked scraggly and dusty. I hated the dry summer fields that surrounded the town, the dust and the hot, relentless wind. I thought seriously about running away, finding my way somehow back to the island.

Autumn was better, with vivid colors and the smell of burning leaves. But the winter was cold and our big old house was drafty. Martin was sick again, and we all thought of the time on the island when he nearly died. Mother went around with her lips pressed tight together much of the time. Father was remote and he had headaches. Nothing was right.

Millicent lived in the house next door. She was tall and thin like me, but she had red hair and very pale skin that was covered with freckles. Her front teeth were crooked, and she sniffed. We became friends.

As far as I could tell, Millicent had no father. At least, he was never around. Her mother was there, vague and fluttery and smelling of something I couldn't identify. Millicent's grandmother, Mrs. Reed, was in charge. She made Millicent's clothes, she baked bread and cleaned the house, and gave orders in a tight, cold voice.

Millicent's cat, called simply Cat, was large, gaunt, mottled gray and yellow, and he was friend to no one. But Millicent was his mistress. She would take Cat up to the top of the stairs, balance him on the railing, and push.

Cat slid down that waxed railing, digging in his claws and screaming all the way. At the bottom he would land on his feet, lay back his ears, and wail. Then Millicent would grab him and take him up to the top again.

I felt sorry for him. But he was Millicent's cat. I'd say, "Millicent, that's mean."

She'd say, "He likes it."

Time went slowly, even after Millicent and I became friends. But spring came and went, and finally it was summer again. I worked most of that summer taking care of pets for people, mowing lawns for our neighbors, picking cherries. I was saving money for my heart's desire. I loved those words: *heart's desire*. Mine was a heavy red sweater with pockets and a shawl collar.

I didn't have much time for Millicent that second summer when we were twelve. I was too busy working. Finally I had enough money for the sweater, and Millicent went with me when I bought it. I wore it to school proudly on a crisp autumn day.

Soon after that Millicent got a red sweater, too, like mine. But hers was just a sweater. She hadn't worked and waited for it.

One day when it was time to go home after school, I went to the hall to get my sweater, and it was gone. I looked everywhere for it. I went back to the classroom to ask Miss Shelby what to do. There was Millicent ready to go home, and she was wearing my sweater.

"Oh Millicent," I cried with relief, "that's my sweater."

She stared at me silently and a chill from her glance froze me.

"Millicent," I said again.

"It's my sweater," she said.

"But you didn't wear yours today," I told her. "I remember. It's mine."

Miss Shelby looked at me, at Millicent, at the sweater. "Are you sure?" she asked me.

"I'm sure."

She asked Millicent, "Could you be mistaken?"

"It's my sweater," Millicent said again.

"You know it isn't yours," I told her. I wanted to say, *You watched me earn it. You saw my blisters. You were with me when I bought it. You were happy for me. Weren't you?*

Then Miss Shelby asked me, "How can you be sure it is yours?"

I said, "Tell her to take it off and I'll show you."

"Please take it off, Millicent," Miss Shelby said.

Without saying a word Millicent took off the sweater and handed it to Miss Shelby. Miss Shelby gave it to me. I turned back the inner flap of the pocket, the secret lining where my mother had embroidered my name. My name. Not Millicent's.

Millicent took a jacket out of the book bag she always carried to school. She put on the jacket and walked away from us, out of the room.

Miss Shelby looked at me. She touched my hand and said, "I'm so sorry." She looked sad and worried. Then she said, "Poor Millicent." I looked at her, puzzled.

At home I went to my father and told him what had happened. "I'll never speak to her again," I said. "She's not my friend."

"But once she was," my father said. "*Nicht war?*"

"I suppose so."

"I know how you must feel," Father said. "It is painful to be betrayed by a friend. Painful past endurance. Still . . ." He leaned back in his chair and looked at me. I felt that he wasn't seeing me anymore. He was thinking about something else.

So I went to my mother and told her. "She didn't have to do it," I said. "She has her own sweater. I hate her."

"It's hard to understand," my mother said. "I wonder why she did it? What do you think?"

"I don't know," I said, not really caring. She had done it. Never mind why.

For days, for weeks I went to school and came home from school alone. I pretended Millicent was a stranger. I didn't speak to her. I didn't look at her. I was miserable.

One day my mother asked me, "Haven't you punished Millicent long enough?"

"Punished her?" I felt betrayed again, by my own mother. "But she lied. She lied to Miss Shelby. She lied to me. And she stole."

My mother sighed. "I know. Poor Millicent."

"Poor Millicent? Why does everybody say 'Poor Millicent'? What about me? Why do you always say 'Poor Millicent'? It isn't fair."

"Of course it isn't fair, and I'm sorry it had to happen. But I'm sorry for Millicent, too. I think she doesn't like herself very much."

"I don't like her, either."

Mother smiled at me. "Sometimes she isn't very likable. But I guess we all have our moments, don't we? It's easy enough to like someone who is likable, I suppose. It's harder to like someone who isn't."

I thought about that for a long time. I thought about Millicent. Her father had left long ago, people said. Millicent never talked about him, but I didn't think he was dead. Just gone. Her mother drifted through the rooms of that house like a ghost. Mrs. Reed never smiled. Even Cat was aloof and angry. As I thought about these things I felt vaguely ashamed.

So one day I went over to Millicent's house and rang the bell. When she came to the door she seemed surprised to see me. "Want to go for a walk?" I asked her.

She stared at me for a while. Then she said, "Sure."

So we spent time together after that, and we went to school and came home together. But it was never quite the same. I wore my red sweater all that winter, but somehow it didn't seem to keep me as warm as it had before.

One day, sitting in our kitchen with cookies and milk, we talked about what we wanted to be when we were older. "I'm going to be a teacher," I said, "and a musician, and I'm going to write books."

"What kind of books?" Millicent asked.

"Books about people."

"Will you write about me?"

"Maybe," I said, although at the moment I thought it unlikely. She was getting over a cold. Her face was even more pinched and sallow than usual and all her freckles stood out. Her hair was limp and stringy. She sniffed a good deal.

"Well," she said, "if you do, make me beautiful and happy. Will you?"

CHAPTER

SEVENTEEN

M y first memories are of snow. I was three when my father pulled me through a sparkling, white world in a small homemade sled. Wrapped in rose-colored warmth, knit by my mother, I felt safe, as if all that whiteness was for me. Later, when I was older, snow still had a quality of mystery and promise. I would go to sleep at night when the trees were stark, the earth brown and dead. I would waken in the morning to a silent, white world, pure and shining. Something had happened while I slept, and it seemed to me that God had made the world beautiful just for me.

I did not realize then that snow can be an enemy. I would walk happily in that white world, bundled up against its chill, and feel that nothing could possibly go wrong, nothing could hurt me in such a secret quiet. All morning I would walk in the snow, coming inside for a while to get warm, to eat Mother's fresh bread and fragrant, steaming soup. Then I would go out again.

And at sunset, those colors! No artist could capture them, I thought. I wanted them to stay, to blazon the sky, but they always faded. I wondered where they went, where God stored them until the next time he needed them. Always, it seemed to me, something marvelous happened when it snowed.

But there was one year when I was truly frightened by my friend, the snow. All during Holy Week the sky had been leaden, the air unmercifully cold. Mother nursed the recalcitrant furnace, her fingers cracked and bleeding from the cold. Martin, lying on the sofa, wheezed and coughed, and I thought of the time he almost died. Father was distant and stern, as he always was during this time of the year.

And then, when I woke up on Good Friday morning, there was a stillness that I had never felt before. It wasn't so much the absence of sound, as the presence of a new element that I could not define. The house seemed laden with a new burden.

I got up and went to the window. I looked out upon a transformed world. Snow lay as far as I could see, almost at eye level, there in my upstairs room. I could see only the roof of the church next door.

I hurried downstairs into the kitchen, where my parents sat drinking coffee. It smelled good. I looked at my father. I had learned long ago not to bother him on Good Friday, but today was different. My mother looked at me and smiled. "We've had a blizzard," she said, "while we slept."

"How deep is the snow?" I asked. "How much is there?"

"Go look out the living-room window," my father said.

I ran to see what he wanted to show me. I looked out the window, but there was only white, dense and powerful. I went to the front door and tried to open it. But I could not.

"Are we snowbound?" I asked, thinking of a poem I had heard in school.

"In a way we are," my mother said. "The telephone lines are down. I guess the snow was too heavy for them. The roads are impassable. We'll just have to wait for the snowplow."

"May I go out?" I asked.

"After breakfast. For a while."

"Me, too?" Martin wheezed.

"I'm afraid not, honey," Mother told him. "We have to keep you warm." And that closed look crossed Martin's face.

So after breakfast I put on my warmest wraps, my mittens, and a muffler, and I helped my father tunnel through the snow into our back yard. We saw the church, its doors blocked with high white drifts.

"Will there be church today?" I asked him.

"I guess not," he said. "Nobody can get through."

So I played in the deepest snow I had ever seen. I pretended I was a traveler, lost in a cold, white wasteland. I pretended that no one could find me. I frightened myself until I had to go inside.

"What will happen to Easter?" I asked my parents. "Will it come anyway? Even in the snow?"

"Easter will come," my father said, "no matter what. Do not be afraid. We will keep Good Friday. It is necessary. And then Easter will find us."

I couldn't understand how that would happen. Father read the Good Friday service to the three of us in the warm living room. It made me sad, but not as sad as I had been that Good Friday on the island when my father was so angry with me. Mother listened, her hands folded in her lap. Martin went to sleep on the sofa. I wondered about the words in one of the psalms. *I waited patiently for the Lord.* Maybe, if we all waited patiently, Easter would come.

My father was right and it did come, although only a few sturdy people dared the trip through deep snow. The air smelled faintly of lilies, I thought, even though there weren't any. But sunlight slanted through the windows and stained-glass colors danced. And it seemed to me that, faintly, I heard angels singing Alleluia.

CHAPTER
EIGHTEEN

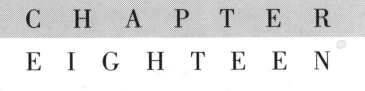

I was up in my room reading Willa Cather's *The Song of the Lark,* walking with her through the land of the Ancient People. On the periphery I heard voices: my father's, thick with anger, Martin's reedy treble voice, begging. I must have been hearing them for some time, but I didn't go to find out what was wrong. I didn't want my summer spell broken. It kept me safe.

But after a while I went down to the kitchen, and Martin was there. He wore his most ragged pair of knee pants, a torn shirt, and dirty tennis shoes. His book bag, lumpy and bulging, was on the table.

"Hi," I said. "Going somewhere?"

His lower lip protruded and his shoulders were stiff. I couldn't see his eyes. He didn't answer me. He opened the icebox door and took out sandwich makings: cold meat, pickles, cheese.

I began slicing bread. The crust was fragrant and crisp. "Where are you going?" I asked him.

He slid an oblique glance from his lowered eyes, watching while I buttered slices of bread, but he didn't answer.

"Do you want pickles on your peanut butter?"

"Yes." It was more a growl than a word. He put oranges in the bookbag, and cookies, crackers and cheese, all in a jumble. Finally, he said, "I'm running away."

I didn't look at him. "How many sandwiches?"

"I don't care."

"How far are you going?"

"I don't know."

"Is Sam going with you?"

"No. He has to go visit his grandmother."

I thought of the sound of two angry voices woven into the fabric of my book. I cut the sandwiches into quarters, the way he liked them. "What happened?" I asked him.

"Nothing."

"Something happened. Don't you want to tell me?" I located my canteen high on the pantry shelf. I chipped off pieces of ice to drop into the canteen to chill it. The ice pick was needle-sharp. Father had taught me how to use it without hurting myself. I began to make lemonade.

Martin chewed at a fingernail, the quick already exposed and raw. "He yelled at me again."

"I know. I heard. What for?"

"He . . . they won't let me join the Cub Scouts. She says I can't because I was sick last winter and I might get sick again because scouts go camping, and stuff. He says not to bother him. They won't listen to me. She just locks up her face and says no and he yells. Sam's going to be a cub. We want to be together. I want it more than anything. They won't let me. I'm running away."

"But where will you go? What will you do? Do you have any money?"

He dug into his pocket and brought up a few pennies, two nickels, a pencil stub, some peanuts, and a jawbreaker, studded with lint. He held out the collection.

"That won't get you very far." I poured lemonade into the canteen.

"I don't care. I'm going. They make me mad. I'm so mad my head hurts."

I looked at him then and thought I saw the beginning of tears. I knew he wouldn't want me to touch him, but I had to do something. Anything.

"Wait here a minute, will you?" I asked him. "I'll be right back." I went to my room and found the new notebook I'd been saving. The covers were blue, the empty lines straight and inviting.

I took it downstairs to Martin. "Here." I handed it to him. "This is what I do when they make me mad. I write down the way I feel. It helps a lot. I do it all the time. Write whatever you want to. No one will see it but you. It will be your private book."

He took it, opening it, looking at the empty pages. "What if I can't spell the words?"

"It doesn't matter," I told him. "Write the way you feel. Draw, if you want to. Just do it. You'll feel better. I know you will."

Still he looked at the book, smoothing its clean, blank pages. His hand was sturdy and brown against the glossy white of the paper. Then he shoved his book bag aside and put the notebook on the table, creasing it so it lay flat. He took the pencil stub from his pocket and licked it. Then he said, "You can see the first thing I write. I want you to see it."

While I watched he wrote his name, printing it carefully in big block letters on the first page. Then he wrote: *Im mad. Im eight years old and they wont let me be a . . .*

He looked up at me. "How do you spell scout?"

I spelled it for him.

He wrote, *Scout. They yell at me. Im running away.*

He put the book in his bag.

"Listen, Martin," I said. "I'll talk to them about it. Being a scout, I mean. Maybe they don't understand how much it means to you. I'll talk to them. Maybe they'll listen."

For a moment his face lit up. Then he scowled and said, "I'm still going to run away." I helped him struggle into the shoulder straps of the bag. It looked heavy. He asked me, "Do you want to come, too?"

"Well," I said, "where would we go?"

"To the badlands."

I didn't like the badlands, out far east of town, and Martin knew it. I had told him I thought hell might be like that: dry, deserted, frightening. But I liked walking on the dry riverbed under cottonwood trees. And it was a good morning for a picnic.

"All right," I said, "I'll go with you. Partway, at least."

CHAPTER

NINETEEN

A t fourteen I was a misfit in almost every way. Because we moved so often I would make a friend only to lose her, settle into a school only to be uprooted and placed in another one. I was taller than any boy or girl in my class, and I was also the youngest. I was miserable in this new town, in this new school, in this new parish.

My father, suffering from the disease that killed him several years later, was impatient, bitter, unkind. I was afraid of him. I did not know then how much he suffered. That knowledge came later.

My mother was unhappy, too, and increasingly stern and aloof. Nine-year-old Martin seemed to move about in a small world of his own and, although I loved him more than anyone else, he would not welcome me into his private world. I did not know then that he was protecting himself in his own way. I learned that later, when it was almost too late.

I had consolations. Music was one, books another. And a vague, mysterious trust in God was another. But, in spite of everything, I was desperately unhappy.

One day I came home after school and, as usual, went to the piano. I had played a few bars of a Chopin nocturne when I was interrupted by my father's angry voice shouting down at me from upstairs.

"Will you stop that infernal racket! I'm trying to study."

I felt bodily harm; the voice was so angry, the tone so violent. A surge of hatred for this man rose in me like gorge. I slammed both my hands down on the keys as hard as I could in a cacophony of shattered chords. Then I ran from the house, slamming the front door.

Weeping tears of rage and desperation, I walked blindly, not caring where I went, not seeing anyone or anything. *Honor thy father and thy mother.* The words pounded in my head as I ran. Guilt piled itself on top of rage and misery. I felt lost and damned.

At last I found myself at the library. I pulled a book from a shelf, the first one I touched, and went to one of the back tables where no one was sitting.

Thoughts chased themselves in my mind. *I'll run away. Where can I go? I don't have anybody. I don't have a place. Who can forgive me? What will become of me?*

After a while I was aware that the librarian, Miss Winfield, stood beside me, a book in one hand, a clean handkerchief in the other. She gave me the handkerchief. I wiped my eyes and blew my nose. She handed me the book. "Remember," she said, "it's practically never as bad as it seems. You'll live through this one, too." Putting the book on the table in front of me, she went back to her desk.

You'll live through this one, too. How much did she know about me, about what was in my mind? I looked at the book. *My Antonia* by Willa Cather. Miss Winfield knew how much I loved Cather's writing. Soon I was engrossed in the book, forgetting everything but the boy Jimmy, discovering his new home in the Nebraska prairie land. And there was the new word from the Bible, spoken by Jimmy's grandfather with such solemnity: *Selah.* Like Jimmy, I did not know what it meant, but it seemed to me that it must be full of mystery and power.

Finally I checked out the book, thanked Miss Winfield, and started home. When I got there I heard my mother and

Martin talking in the kitchen. I did not know where my father was, and I hoped I could avoid him.

Slowly, I started up the stairs toward my own room, not yet ready to speak to anyone. I stood for a moment on the small landing, midway up the curving stairs. Someone before us had installed a small stained-glass window there. *God*, I thought, *if you are there, and if you care about me, please give me some kind of a sign. Just give me a sign. Please.*

I do not know what I expected. Lightning, on this clear day? Voices in the silence? An angel hovering directly in front of me?

I have never forgotten that moment. It has become a talisman for me, a touchstone during all the years. As I stood there alone, two things happened simultaneously. A shaft of light pierced the stained glass, showering prisms on the landing, and a meadowlark sang somewhere, clear and sweet. Light and song mingled. I was caught in beauty.

And then my father appeared at the top of the landing. Neither of us spoke. My heart pounded as I walked up toward him. When we were face to face I saw his eyes, behind the thick lenses of his glasses. They were dark with pain.

"Forgive me," he said quietly. "Forgive me, if you can. I am truly sorry."

"Oh, Father," I said, hearing the love and anguish in his voice. "Oh, Father." And we embraced, there at the top of the stairs.

Color and sound and love followed me into my bedroom under the sloping roof, and once again I felt safe.

Selah.

CHAPTER

T W E N T Y

One January day I walked through the park to my piano lesson, my head full of the sweetness of the Chopin nocturne I'd been memorizing. A gentle snow fell, lying on the ground, along branches of trees, and on the roof of the bandstand where summer concerts were held. The snow covered all the dark places on the ground and the darkness within me, as well: shadows caused by my father's angry words, my mother's discontent, and by my fears for Martin, who was changing, even toward me.

It was music that comforted me most during those dark South Dakota years. Poetry and music. And Professor Kohler. The Professor was a highly respected musician who had come to teach in our college town. On the day I went to play for him, to see if he would accept me as a pupil, I was terrified. With clammy hands and with my heart pounding so hard that I could see the front of my dress move, I rang his bell.

He came at once. Taking my hand, he drew me into the room. "Come in. Come in. I have been looking forward to hearing you play."

His accent was German, like my father's. He wore a plum-colored velvet jacket. His thick white hair waved back from a high forehead, and his white mustache was neatly trimmed. His eyes, set under white brows, were luminous and kind. I forgot to stoop a bit, as I usually did, to conceal at least some part of my sixty-nine inches. I stood tall and looked into his eyes.

"*Ach*," he smiled. "I do admire tall girls. You do not mind my saying so? Like princesses, they are, so regal."

My classmates, over whom I towered, had nicknamed me *The Monument*.

The Professor looked at my hands. "Such nice hands you have, too. Good strong hands. Truly, hands for the piano. Come now. Come and play for me."

Now, at the Professor's house I opened the door quietly and went in. Someone was playing part of a Beethoven sonata. I put my gloves in the pocket of my coat and hung it on the hall rack. I brushed the snow off my hair and blew on my fingers to warm them. The Beethoven sounded rich and mysterious, and I wondered who was playing.

I went into the music room and sat in the big shabby armchair in the corner. "The Visitor's Chair," Professor Kohler called it. A young man I had not seen before was playing a movement from the *Waldstein*. His eyes were closed. He sat erect and still, hardly moving his body. Only the music moved, filling the room and warming it.

I closed my eyes, too, and listened. But soon I had to look at the pianist again. His dark hair was thick and curly. He looked as if he might be tall. I hoped so.

When he had finished the movement he was playing he paused. The Professor said, "*Ja*, I think Beethoven would be pleased. Beethoven, himself." Then he noticed me and said, "Julie, come. Come meet Nathan."

The young man stood beside the piano. I had been right. He was tall. He was not exactly handsome. His features were irregular, his mouth too large, his nose a bit crooked. But his dark eyes were clear and direct, and he looked at me as if I were a real person. He held out his hand. I put my own into it, and his clasp was firm and warm.

"Your hand is cold," he said. "It took me half my lesson time to get my own hands warmed up, didn't it, Professor?" He rubbed my right hand in both his own. Then he turned away and said, "Thank you, sir. I really enjoyed the hour. Tomorrow at the same time, then?"

"Good," the Professor said. "The same time."

When he had gone I asked, "Who is he? I thought I knew all your students."

"He is a visitor," Professor Kohler told me. "His family is here from Connecticut. His father spends the next months working in our hospital. He is a specialist in pediatrics, Nathan tells me. He and our Dr. Fields do a research project here together. Very unusual. The family stays, I believe, only through the summer. Nathan goes to Julliard in the fall. I have the pleasure of teaching him in the meantime so he does not interrupt his study."

The fall was half a year away, and besides, I hardly heard what the Professor said. I only knew that suddenly I was changed. The hand Nathan had warmed in his own now had a special kind of warmth, and the Chopin nocturne took on a new poetry. I had never played so easily.

When I had finished playing the nocturne the Professor said, "I have had a splendid day. Two successes in one afternoon. Nathan plays Beethoven as if he had conceived the sonata himself. You play Chopin with a new maturity. Am I a far better teacher than even I knew?"

He was teasing me, but I didn't care. My hands knew exactly what to do all the rest of the hour, and when my time was up I was amazed. It had gone so fast.

I was not exactly surprised when I stepped out into the early twilight and found Nathan waiting. He was bareheaded and the collar of his coat was pulled high around his chin.

"Aren't you cold?" I asked him. "Have you been waiting all this time?"

"No. I've been walking." His hands were deep in his pockets. "I love to walk after my lesson. I'm always too excited to be quiet. Music excites me. You, too?"

"Yes." We looked at each other. He took my right hand and held it, putting both our hands in the pocket of his coat. "I'd like to walk home with you. I want to know where you live."

So we walked together. The sky was streaked with rose and purple, and the snow reflected the colors. The air was still. The breath from our mouths mingled and rose.

Suddenly he asked me, "How old are you?"

"I was sixteen my last birthday." I studied his face again. "You're older, aren't you?"

"A bit."

At my house I asked, "Would you like to come in?"

"Thanks. Not today. Soon, though." He brushed the snow off my collar and off my hair. "Good-bye," he said. "I'll see you again."

That year I was a freshman in the junior college in our town. The great depression dictated our lives, and the tacit knowledge that I would have to earn my own living as soon as possible set my direction for me. I would finish the two-year college course and look for a teaching job.

One evening shortly after I had met Nathan I asked my parents, "What if I could get a scholarship to Julliard?"

Father said, "I thought it was all decided? That you complete two years of college here?"

"I know. But what if I could?"

My parents looked at each other. It was Mother who finally spoke. "I wish we could help you. But we don't have the money. We couldn't even get you to New York for the auditions. I'm sorry, but that's the way it is."

Father said, "*Ja*, I, too, am sorry."

"It's all right," I said. "I understand." I tried to understand, but I didn't want it to be true.

The months unfolded *legato, leggiere*. I thought about Nathan all the time. I remembered the way my hand had felt when he held it, that cold day when we first met. I imagined touching his thick, black hair. I imagined kissing him. I often went early to my lesson so that I could be in the same room with him. I thought he looked at me in a special way, as if he were touching me.

One day when Nathan had played a Brahms intermezzo the Professor said, "You give us great joy with your music, Nathan. We will miss you when you leave us."

And I thought, *No. Don't talk about that. Don't.* I consoled myself with the thought of summer. I would be out of school, and Nathan and I could spend more time together. We could have picnics down by the river, and we could swim. Maybe we could go to Vermillion to hear a concert. My mind led me into infinite possibilities.

One Friday evening in late April Nathan played a recital at the Professor's house for a group of students and friends. As I listened I was taken into a new dimension of time. Nathan was on one side of the universe, among turning planets, in a different galaxy. I was here, caught forever on earth.

I can't say good-bye to him, I thought. *I can't. Maybe he doesn't know that I love him. Maybe I should tell him. He must feel the same way about me. He just hasn't told me. I'll tell him. I'll tell him tonight.*

But after the concert Nathan was caught in a crowd of admiring people. He smiled at me as I waited to speak to him. When it was my turn all I could say was, "You played beautifully."

He started to speak, but a large woman in a green voile dress spoke first. I had watched her take a fan of ivory and silk from her purse before Nathan began to play. She fanned herself gently all evening, keeping time with his music. Now I heard her say, "My dear young man . . ."

I knew there would be no chance to be alone with him so I walked home, past bushes of bridal wreath heavy with blossoms, through aisles of lilac trees, their scent enveloping me like music.

I had trouble sleeping that night. I lay half-dreaming. I saw myself magically transported to New York with Nathan, living there, a part of his world, a part of his life.

I slept late the next morning. When I woke I thought, *Today's Saturday. We'll walk through the park and I'll tell him. Then he'll tell me, and something wonderful will happen.*

While I was eating breakfast Nathan called. "Listen, Julie. I have to talk fast."

Suddenly I was afraid.

"Our plans have changed. I was going to tell you last night but there was no chance. All those people. The woman with the fan. You know? My parents have suddenly decided to go to Europe. My father has finished his work here sooner than he thought he would. I'm going with them.

"The Professor knows Gieseking. Did you know that? He and my father were finally able to arrange a trans-Atlantic telephone call, and Gieseking has agreed to teach me this summer. I can hardly believe my luck. Then, after Germany, I'll go straight to New York in September."

"When are you leaving?" My mouth was so dry I could hardly form the words.

"Right away. Today. I'll always remember you as a special friend. You and the Professor saved this winter for me. You'll never know how much I dreaded coming to South Dakota. I'll miss you both. I couldn't leave without telling you good-bye."

He was gone. I went up to my room before anyone could see me and ask questions. I sat at my desk and looked out the window at the tops of the trees. I could catch the scent of apple blossoms.

I tried not to think of Nathan's words. I tried not to think of him at all. I turned away from the window and looked around my room. What was I searching for?

A book of Millay's poems was on my bedside table. My Bible was there, too. It had been a gift from my parents on my eighth birthday. Its covers were soft black leather, and my name was embossed in gold.

I picked it up. I'll ask for a sign, I thought. Whatever I open to will be a sign. Not looking at it, I let the Bible fall open. Then I looked at the page and read, "And the sons of Eliphaz were Teman, Omar, Zepho, and Gatam and Kenag."

I tried again. "Zedekia was one and twenty years old when he began to reign, and he reigned seven years in Jerusalem."

I sighed and shut the book. But soon I opened it again, chose the place, and read:

As the apple tree among the trees of the wood, so is my beloved among the sons. I sat down under his shadow with great delight, and his fruit was sweet to my taste. He brought me to the banqueting house, and his banner over me was love. Stay me with flagons, comfort me with apples; for I am sick of love.

I knew I would never see Nathan again. He had known it all winter. I wondered if grief and love always went together. Quite suddenly I thought of my parents. I saw them in a new way. I saw them not only as my mother and father, but as a man and a woman who were separate from me: a man and a woman who had once loved each other. They must have, once. Now they were alienated, lonely, unhappy.

Each one of us was alone in this house where we lived as a family: my father, my mother, my brother, and I. Each one was alone and miserable.

When I finally let myself cry, that spring morning in my room under the sloping roof, I cried for all of us.

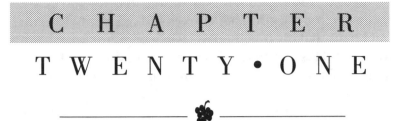

T W E N T Y • O N E

I t is possible that my father was the only man in our small South Dakota town who had a Ph.D. He had earned it at Heidelberg, and no dueling scar ever carried more honor for its owner than those letters behind my father's name.

When I graduated from junior college at the age of eighteen, I was carrying on a family tradition that education was more important than anything except, perhaps, cleanliness and godliness.

I was a good student. That was expected of me. During my school years the dates I had were most often with boys who called to ask whether they could come over so that I could help them with Latin. Or French. Or English. Or ancient history.

My father was invited to give the college graduation address, and the ceremony was held in the Methodist Church because the high-school auditorium was too small to hold everyone.

On that day we entered to the inevitable sounds of *Pomp and Circumstance,* played on the church organ, and we sat in the choir loft facing the audience. It seemed to me that the whole town was there. I saw my mother with Martin beside her. He was there, I knew, sullenly, under protest. I looked for Professor Kohler, and he nodded to me when our eyes met.

I had a sense of foreboding. My father had been withdrawn and silent all morning, with one of his headaches.

He had, of course, congratulated me, and he and Mother had given me my gift. That book is still one of my treasures, but I never handle it without a feeling of grief. Can it be true that objects sometimes retain and carry with them the quality of strong emotion that once surrounded them?

After an introduction by Mr. Ames, the president of the board of education, my father stood to begin his address. He wore his street clericals, and he looked, as always, imposing and serious. Although I had asked him what his topic would be, he had not told me.

"It will be an important address," he had said. "Trust me."

I wanted to trust him.

For several long moments my father stood quietly before he began to speak. Then he said, "And there was war in heaven: Michael and his angels fought against the dragon; and the dragon fought and his angels."

He began by telling us, the graduating class, that we would all have battles to fight in the life ahead of us, and that we must fight them on the side of the angels. I could accept that.

Then he cautioned us about any fears or reservations we might have in facing the changes that were sure to await all of us.

"Science tells us that everything moves," he said. "Atoms, neutrons, particles all move. Our planet moves. It hurtles through space, moving, rushing through eternal Time. It is the nature of things to move. In the book of Genesis we read, . . . 'and the Spirit of God moved . . .' "

I found these ideas exciting, and I thought about them while he continued to speak. When I returned from my own thoughts to his words I sensed a change in him and in his audience. I realized that he had, quite suddenly, changed his subject. He had begun to speak about the inhumanity of Man. And for an eternity he spoke out against the inhumanity that had been shown to him during the war days. He became irrational. He shouted and he harangued those people who had not even known what his early agonies had been. And as if he were speaking to his persecutors, he held us all responsible.

"You hypocrites, you whited sepulchers," he shouted. "You sit there smug and comfortable and you do not know the evil you have brought upon me. You have not been your brother's keeper. You have crossed over to the other side while I lay wounded and bleeding."

I prayed, *Lord, if you love me, let me die now.* But I didn't die. My heart pounded until I thought I would suffocate from the noise in my ears. The girl sitting beside me reached out and took my hand. Our hands were welded together, and I think she must bear scars from my fingernails.

I looked at my mother. She sat with her eyes closed, her face drawn and colorless. Martin got up and left the church. I watched him walk away, his back stiff, hands thrust deep into the pockets of his best gray trousers, his blond head bent slightly forward, as if he were following it. *He looks like an old man,* I thought. *No thirteen-year-old boy should ever have to look like that.*

After a while Father stopped speaking and sat down. Somehow the ceremony was concluded. We were given our diplomas, and when Mr. Ames handed me my own his eyes were compassionate and he touched me lightly on the shoulder. We all marched down the center aisle of that church, on our way out to take our places in the world. I looked at my mother as I passed her, but her eyes were still closed. I didn't look at anyone else.

In the robing room I took off my cap and gown and, as we had been instructed, left them with Mr. Warden, our math teacher. I didn't meet his eyes, but he said, "Congratulations, Julie. You are a fine student, and it has been a privilege to teach you."

I wanted to thank him but I couldn't speak. I left the church, not waiting for my mother, not trying to find Martin. I walked in the opposite direction from home, through the park, past the band stand, to the Professor's house. I waited there on the dusty front step, not caring whether I soiled the skirt of my new white dress.

When he came, he opened the door and we went in together. He went to the kitchen and came back in a moment with two crystal goblets and a decanter on a silver tray. He poured a small amount of golden wine in each goblet. He handed one to me. Then he raised his own glass and said, "My homage to you on this important day. May you dwell in the knowledge that you are held in high regard by those who know you. I salute you."

I sipped my wine. Then I asked, "Will you play for me, please?"

He played Bach inventions and partitas and the cool, clean architecture of that music brought me a measure of peace. When he had finished he stood and held out his hands to me. "And now," he said, helping me up, "you must go home. Your mother and your brother need you. You are stronger than you know. Go home. And remember that your father needs you, too."

I started to speak, but he put his fingers against my lips. "It is true. He needs you."

"I wish you were my father," I told the Professor.

"I am, *liebling*," he said. "I am your father in music. Now go home. Go home."

I held his hand against my cheek for just a moment before I left him.

CHAPTER
TWENTY • TWO

A t eighteen how does one learn to forgive? Caught in a trap set by circumstance, I thought that I would never forgive my father, no matter what anyone said. Each time I went downtown, each time I went to church, I thought people looked at me furtively and whispered to each other.

Since graduation day Father had retreated into his study where he spent most of his time. Martin was seldom at home. Mother resembled pictures I had seen of carved figureheads on ships—stern, rigid, noble, facing into danger.

Yet, in spite of everything, sometimes I thought I could not contain all the love I felt for this family of mine, and my hopeless, desperate desire that we could be happy.

And then I got a letter from Mr. Hart, superintendent of the schools in Riverview, a small town about thirty miles west of home. My application had been accepted. I had been hired to teach the fifth and sixth grades.

"That's wonderful," Mother said when I showed her the letter. I heard the relief in her voice. "I'm so proud of you. Go tell your father. He'll be proud, too."

I really didn't want to talk to him, but I knew I should. I knocked on the door of his study.

"Come."

I went in and said abruptly, "I've got a job." I held the letter out to him. "Mother wanted me to tell you."

He read the letter and handed it back to me. "So. We now have a professor daughter. I congratulate you."

Something in his voice reminded me of the way he had been when I was a child and had pleased him. I wanted to cry, but I did not. I just stood there awkwardly.

"Will you sit with me for a while?" He motioned to the chair across from his own. I sat down, feeling uneasy. He said, "May we talk together, you and I? There has been much on my mind and in my heart to tell you. But I have not quite had the courage to speak. If you will help me, I will try to explain what happened to me on the day of your graduation."

I would have liked to say, *It's all right, Father.* But it wasn't and I couldn't say it.

"I do not really know what happened to me," he said. I knew he was groping for words. "For a while I was saying what I had planned to say. Then suddenly I had no more control over what I was saying than I had had over the events about which I spoke."

For a long moment he was silent. Then he continued. "It is a terrifying thing, to be out of control. Most of my life I have been unable to control the things that happen to me. Neither have I been able to control my reactions to those things.

"Often I have prayed. 'Set thou a seal upon my lips.' But no one hears me. It is as if I suffer from a terrible, festering inner wound that suddenly ruptures, spewing poison on anyone who is near me."

He looked so desolate that I thought, *Oh Father. What can I say to you?* Still, I said nothing.

"How can I possibly ask you to forgive me?" My father spoke to me across a great chasm. "I cannot forgive myself."

We looked at each other, my father and I. I felt as if I were the parent and he the child, waiting to be comforted. Then I thought of something. "Do you remember the time when I stepped on a needle? Mother blamed herself. She said it was all her fault?"

"I remember. Of course I remember."

"You told Mother that she had to forgive herself. You said that was more important even than forgiving someone else."

"My God, how long ago that was. How long. In another life. Yet it might have been yesterday. How could I not remember?"

I waited.

After a while Father spoke again. "Today. Yesterday. This life. Another life. I have come to believe that we do not fully comprehend the meaning of Time. We are human and fallible. We exist in time that we experience with our limited, finite lives. That kind of time, man's time, is called *chronos*. It is the time we pass and lose and waste and kill. You understand? In *chronos* you are my young daughter whom I have injured. We both suffer."

I knew he was thinking out loud and did not expect me to answer.

"But *kairos* is God's time, infinite, boundless. In it all things are possible. Even for me, perhaps. In *kairos* I may at last become the man I wish to be: loving, wise, compassionate, forgiving.

"Truly, I do not mean to excuse myself for the pain I have caused my family. I only wish you to know that I seem too weak to help myself. But I will try, Julie. I will try. Perhaps it will be possible, in some holy time, to be as we once were, long ago."

As he talked I remembered some of those times, the way we once were, the first time I held Martin, when Father put him in my arms. My first shiny black slippers and my bubble pipe. The day of my new glasses, when I saw clearly for the first time.

For an instant it was like that now; a clear, new vision. I started to speak, but Father said, "I must tell you one thing more. Your mother and brother and I must go away at the end of summer. I am no longer to have a parish. The bishop has kindly arranged for me a part-time teaching job at a school in Vermillion. I shall teach, as I did once, German and Philosophy."

"But, Father . . ."

"*Ja*. I know. We will be separated. For the first time. But it will be all right. We will be parted by miles, but we will be together, bound by love, no matter where we are. For you have taken a step toward understanding. I can see it in your eyes. We will hold this moment fast while we are parted, you and I."

I went to him then, and kissed his cheek.

CHAPTER

TWENTY · THREE

❦

s the time came closer for me to go one way and
my family another, I grew less sure that I really
understood my father's ideas about Time. They
seemed terribly involved. I was not a philosopher. I was a
frightened girl, not yet a woman, and I was fearful, in-
secure, and ambivalent in my feelings.

Shortly before Labor Day we parted. My parents and
Martin drove off toward Vermillion in our old car after they
had put me on the train to Riverview.

Listening to the rhythmic sounds of the train I watched
the countryside rush past the smudged windows. Trees
merged with telephone poles. Large patches of farmland
merged with the horizon. Once a little boy in overalls
waved as the train passed. *He wishes he were on this train*, I
thought, and I waved back. I looked at clusters of houses.
People live in them, I told myself, *families. They aren't even
aware of me. I'm alone. A stranger. And I'll be alone among
strangers when I arrive in Riverview*. Thinking of my family
driving in the opposite direction while I rode out of the
circle of their lives, I struggled to stay calm.

Toward noon when the train pulled into the station, it
stopped just long enough to unload me and my luggage.
Then it whistled its long, lonely sound and rushed on
toward Denver. I stood by the red frame station, hearing the
wheels as they repeated *Good-bye, good-bye, good-bye*.

When I couldn't see the train any longer I looked
around me. The grain elevator towered like a giant against

the blazing September sky. I saw the corrugated metal roof of the Feed Store, heat waves shimmering above it. But I saw no one at all. I felt as if I were the last person alive on a strange and hostile planet.

Then a pickup truck pulled into the station yard, raising clouds of dust, and someone got out and hurried toward me.

"Miss Erlich?" His voice was deep and resonant, his eyes vividly blue. He was taller than I and somewhat older, too, I thought. He wore brown trousers and a blue shirt, open at the throat. He looked strong. "Miss Julie Erlich?" he asked again.

"Yes, I'm Julie Erlich."

"I'm Todd Ashton. Mr. Hart planned to meet you, but he was called away. I hope you won't mind riding up to Mrs. Larson's with me in the truck."

"Mrs. Larson's?"

"Didn't Mr. Hart tell you? She has a room to rent and he thought it might suit you. Do you have any more luggage?"

He had been loading my suitcases into the back of the truck as he talked. He lifted the heavy bags without effort. I wondered how old he was. He was a man, not a boy. I was sure of that.

"My trunk should be somewhere." I looked around me.

"I'll get it." In a moment he came out of the station with my trunk on a luggage cart. He helped me into the passenger seat saying again, "I'm sorry about the truck, but I thought we'd need it for your things."

As we drove north on Main Street, Todd pointed out buildings to me. "That's the store where I work. That's Thompson's Café, across from the pool hall. Mrs. Thompson's a good cook. Most of the teachers eat there. There's the post office."

"I'll be watching for mail from home," I said. "This is my first time away from my family." It was easy to talk to this man. He was relaxed and friendly.

"Well," he said, "we'll try to keep you busy enough so that you won't get too homesick." Pulling up to the curb he said, "Here we are. Mr. Hart told Mrs. Larson we'd be coming along. She's a bit strange but she's a good person. You'll be safe here, if you decide to stay."

I looked at the old three-story house that was almost hidden behind catalpa trees, lilac bushes, and a formidable assortment of shrubs. Windows, balconies, and small doors were scattered at random in front of the facade. It looked like the witch's house in *Hansel and Gretel*.

Mrs. Larson came to the door when Todd knocked. White hair flew in crazy wisps around her wrinkled face. She had hardly any teeth and her back was distinctly humped. I felt that I would surely be caught in a fairy tale, living in that house.

"Well, Todd, it took you long enough to get here," her voice rasped. "Dawdlin', was you? I heard the train come in. Now, Miss," she spoke without looking at me, "you and me will look at the tower room."

Feeling suddenly reluctant, I glanced at Todd. He smiled and nodded. "I'll wait for you here on the porch."

"Come in, come in." Mrs. Larson's tone was scornful. "You set and wait right there." She pointed to a large chair that had lace antimacassars on the arms.

She led me up steep, winding stairs to a room at the top of the house. It was large, as wide as the house itself, and the roof sloped even more than in my room at home. A bed stood under the slope of the roof, and a desk and chair were placed near a row of windows that overlooked the street. I looked out through thick meshing of branches, and felt once more a part of my own lost childhood.

I saw that the room was lined with doors. I counted twenty, each with a doorknob of a different design. The doors themselves did not match. No two were the same shape.

"Them's my cupboards," Mrs. Larson said. "My Lars believed in never wastin' nothin'. Them doors was left over from houses he built. You won't be needin' them. I've cleaned out these two for you." She showed me two deep closets, each as large as a small room.

"Five dollars a month. Take it or leave it." Her voice scratched like fingernails on a blackboard. "You won't find a better room in this town, no matter what anybody tells you."

I hesitated but she didn't seem to expect me to speak. "You a God-fearin', church-goin' Christian woman?"

"Yes." My throat felt dry.

"Good. Then there won't be no problems. One more thing. You entertain men friends in the parlor, not up here. That clear?"

"Yes, ma'am." Friends? *Men* friends?

As if she read my thoughts she said, "You may not have any yet, but you will soon enough. This town's full of prowlers just watchin' and waitin' for young school teachers." She went downstairs ahead of me, her slippers shuffling, her long blue gingham dress brushing against each step.

Looking over her shoulder she said, "Todd Ashton, now. Him I trust. He'll do you nicely if you're lookin' for a husband."

"I'm not."

"Yes, he'll do you nicely. I've known him since the day he was born. Never gave nobody a minute's trouble in all his twenty-two years."

Todd rose as we came into the parlor. Before he had a chance to speak Mrs. Larson said, "She'll do. I wouldn't have just anybody here, you know. Not in Lars' house. But this one will do."

"I thought you'd say that, Mrs. Larson," Todd said. "Now the question is, does she think the tower room will do?"

"Of course she does. Go get her trunk. And be careful how you drag it up the stairs. Don't go scratchin' the paint and woodwork."

Was I to have nothing to say about deciding my own future? I glanced at Todd. His eyes were amused. I heard myself say, almost as if to challenge him, "It will be fine. I like the tower room."

Todd brought my trunk in on a mover's dolly. He took it upstairs, maneuvering it deftly around the turns. Mrs. Larson's voice followed us. "You stay up there just long enough to set that trunk down, Todd Ashton."

When he had placed the trunk, he asked, "Is there anything else I can do for you while I'm here? Pound nails? Hang pictures? Anything at all? Mrs. Larson won't really mind."

"No," I said, "but thanks." I felt embarrassed as I asked him, "May I pay you for your trouble?"

"Oh, that's okay," he said. "I was glad to do it. I'll see you, I imagine, from time to time."

From time to time. As I lay in bed that night, hearing the dry leaves brush against my window screen, I thought about Time. I remembered the things my father had said. Man's time, God's time. I wished that I had a deeper understanding of these things, for I felt myself to be on the edge of still another kind of time. The time of my own future, the time in which I might find a new kind of identity, separated from the three people who knew me best. Father had said we would always be connected, even though we were apart. Was I caught in a paradox? Drowsy, comfortable, half-praying, half-dreaming, I closed my eyes.

CHAPTER
TWENTY • FOUR

I remember the first time I saw Miranda. It was in church my very first Sunday in Riverview, the day before I started teaching. I sat alone, toward the back of the church. I was conscious of peripheral glances from children and their parents. I could feel them thinking, Is *that* the new teacher? She looks awfully young.

Trying to be casual, to look as if nothing concerned me, I studied the building and the congregation. The inside of the church was as pleasant as its red brick exterior. It was plain and restful. Stained glass windows filtered the sun, and prisms of red and blue touched the walls at random.

I wondered how many of the children would be my students, and how many of the adults were their parents. The word *solid* came to me. These men and women looked solid, as if, through their contact with the earth, they had absorbed some of its reality.

And then I noticed Miranda. She sat alone in a pew ahead of me and to the side. She was small and thin. Her hair was cropped short, and she made me think of a nervous bird. I couldn't decide how old she was. She could have been fifty or ninety.

She sang during the hymns. But the rest of the time, sitting there motionless, she cried. Her tears fell and she didn't even wipe them away. She just sat there, silently crying.

After that I saw her often, wandering around town, wearing a ragged old sweater and tennis shoes, and carrying a big diaper bag. I'd see her talking to the primary children on the playground at school, or looking in the store windows on Main Street. And every Sunday I saw her in church.

I remember our first conversation. She was standing in front of Gilbert's department store. Gilbert's carried a bit of everything: clothing, toys, gifts, yardage, furniture, and things for infants. On this day there was a bassinet in the window, and the doll lying in it looked lifelike. Miranda was talking to it.

I paused beside her. She turned to me and said, "The baby's sweet, isn't he? They take good care of him, I guess." Then she talked to the doll again, smiling and waggling her fingers at it.

And I remember the day I went into the school gym after the boys had finished basketball practice. The gym doubled as an auditorium, and sometimes I played the piano there, just for my own pleasure.

On this late afternoon I heard a Mozart sonata. I went in quietly to see who was playing. It was Miranda. Her eyes were closed and she was completely absorbed in the music. I was surprised and, somehow, almost sad to hear her playing so beautifully.

One day I went into the drugstore and the owner was talking to Miranda. She was holding out two nursing bottles and he said, "Now Miranda, you know you really don't want to buy those. Why don't you put them back on the shelf and get something you need for yourself?" His voice was kind.

"I do need these. You know I do," she insisted. She reached into the diaper bag she carried like a purse and took out a checkbook. She wrote a check and handed it to him. "There you are, Mr. Kocheck," she said.

Mr. Kocheck took the check, put the bottles in a bag, and handed her the package. "Thank you, Miranda," he said. When she left he stared after her and I heard him sigh. He turned to me then and asked, "Can I help you, Miss?"

I was curious. "Can you tell me about her, Mr. Kocheck? I've been wondering about her ever since the first day I saw her. I see her around town all the time, everywhere. Once I heard her playing the piano in the gym at school. I was amazed. She was playing Mozart."

"Poor Miranda," he said. "She grew up here in Riverview. She was always musical. Her folks took her all the way to Vermillion for her piano lessons. She used to practice summer evenings with the windows open. I was moonstruck, I guess. I'd sit on the porch swing all evening, as long as she played, just listening to her. Lots of people listened. She brightened up this town.

"She married young, though, awfully young. Some folks said it was because she had to, you know." Mr. Kocheck seemed embarrassed. "But they married. And then, a couple months before the baby was due to be born, her husband was killed in the field when he got crushed under a tractor.

"Poor Miranda," he said again. "First her husband and then the baby. She lost it. She was terribly sick after that. When she got well again, she was still sick in her mind. Her folks finally had to take her to Yankton. That's the State Hospital, you know."

"I know."

"Well, they let her out after a while and she came back here to live with her folks. Her husband's folks wouldn't have anything to do with her." He paused, staring into the past. "Some folks have queer notions about things, I guess. Anyway, she goes around looking for her baby, buying things for it. She's never accepted any of it, you know: her husband's death, the baby.

"It was years ago, of course. She's been in and out of Yankton a dozen times, I guess. When her parents died she

125

went to live with Mrs. Baker there at the end of Second Street on the edge of town. She's been there ever since. She seems harmless enough. Mrs. Baker will bring back the bottles. The check's no good, of course."

"That's so sad, Mr. Kocheck."

"It's sad, all right. Personally, I don't think she should be out wandering around. But the state takes care of her expenses, and Mrs. Baker is good to her. I suppose she's happier here in her hometown than she would be shut up at Yankton. But it isn't much of a life, is it?"

"No. It isn't."

That December the whole school was involved in preparing the annual Riverview Christmas concert. I was in charge of the elementary school music.

Part of the town tradition was to have the family with the youngest baby take the part of the Holy Family. That year it was to be Marvel's parents with her six-month-old brother, Timmie. Everyone in my class was excited about it. "I hope he doesn't cry," Marvel worried.

"It won't matter if he does," I told her. "All babies cry."

The concert was on a Friday night, and that afternoon we had one last rehearsal. After the children left I stayed in the gym for a while. I sorted music, moved chairs, and saw that everything was ready for the performance. While I was moving the wooden manger Miranda came in. She walked up to the manger and looked at it. I thought she seemed tense.

"He hasn't come yet," she said. "I guess I'll come back tonight."

Faint uneasiness stirred in me, but I was caught up in my own responsibilities. I walked down Schoolhouse Hill in the snow that winter twilight, after Miranda had gone. The lights had come on and I thought Riverview looked like a town under a Christmas tree.

I had supper at Thompson's Café with some of the other teachers. The Thompsons had decorated a small tree and they had hung pleated paper bells, red and green, from the ceiling. Everything looked festive and we laughed together, and were happy. Most of us were going home for Christmas.

When I got back to school that evening, ready to begin the concert, I had almost forgotten about Miranda. Parents and children began to come in, shaking the snow off their coats, stamping the snow off their boots. The parents sat in a circle around the manger, the children gathered together in their places. A sense of anticipation filled the room.

The concert moved smoothly toward its climax. Then Marvel's parents walked the length of the room, through the circle of watchers. Marvel's mother put Timmie in the manger and she sat in a chair beside him. Marvel's father stood, looking proud and happy. Timmie lay waving his fists and contentedly blowing bubbles.

The youngest children gathered around the crèche to sing "Away in a Manger." They stood for a long moment, engrossed in the live baby. He recognized his sister and reached toward her, gurgling happily. Marvel grinned.

Then, just as I began to play it happened. Miranda uncoiled suddenly, like a spring. I hadn't even known she was there, not consciously. But immediately I knew what was happening. I saw her go to the crèche. I saw her pick up the baby and hold him in her arms. I saw her radiant face. Instantly everyone froze. It was a Christmas tableau with a grotesque difference.

Then Timmie cried and his mother took him from Miranda. Miranda's hands reached and she said, "But he came to me at Christmas. He came to me at Christmas."

Mr. Hart and Mrs. Baker came toward Miranda then, and we watched them walk out of the gym, Miranda twisting to look over her shoulder at Timmie.

I saw the children's eyes, large and troubled. And behind my own eyes forever, the sight of Miranda's empty, reaching hands.

CHAPTER
TWENTY · FIVE

T hat first year I taught in Riverview I felt alternately centuries older or years younger than my pupils.

That was the year the Midwest began to blow away. Our first dust storm came up one afternoon at about two o'clock. We had been working on spelling. The children were studying their words when all at once it was too dark to see.

"What's happened?" Stanley asked, forgetting to raise his hand.

We looked toward the north windows. The light had stopped. It was brown out there, dark brown. And it was silent. None of us had ever known anything like this.

One of the children began to whimper. "The sun went out," she said.

I went over and touched her. "It's all right, Lou," I said, trying to believe it. "It's all right."

"But what is it?" Stanley asked again.

"It's dust," Leonard told us. "My dad said this was going to happen. It's dust. Now we won't have any wheat."

Mr. Hart, the principal, came into the room looking serious and grim. "Nobody is to leave until an adult comes for him," he told me. "Don't let anyone leave."

"Yes, sir," I said. But I thought, *Who's going to come for me?*

"Maybe it will never get light again," Marvel said.

"It will, Marvel," I told her, forcing myself to sound positive. "The sun is still there, even though we can't see it.

You just have to believe it. It's really there. You can count on it."

It was still daytime dark with the dust blowing when all the children had finally left. I started down the schoolhouse hill alone with a scarf covering my nose and mouth, trying not to breathe in the dust.

Suddenly headlights loomed like exotic eyes in the dark, and a truck stopped beside me. Todd Ashton called, "Hi. Get in and I'll drive you home."

I sat beside him. He turned the truck around and headed down the hill. "I'm certainly glad to see you," I said. "Have you ever seen anything like this?"

"No. Not like this." His voice was calm, matter-of-fact. "Usually we've had high wind with the dust. But this is sort of spooky, isn't it, with the air so still?"

"It really is. The children were afraid." I glanced at him. "I was, too."

"It's something to be afraid of." He peered into the dark, driving slowly. He pulled up beside Mrs. Larson's house and then he walked to the door with me. "Don't try to go out until it's cleared, will you?"

"I won't. Thank you very much for the ride," I said. "I'm glad you came."

He smiled at me, his eyes startlingly blue. "Any time."

Inside, Mrs. Larson was rocking in the dark in her chair by the window. "It's the end of the world. It's judgment day," she keened, over and over.

It wasn't though. The dust settled, the sun came out, and there was all that dirt to clean up.

Only a few weeks later Wesley died. He was at school one day getting into mischief, doing short division, playing baseball, and the next day he was dead.

"He got drowned swimming in the gravel pit," one of the boys told us. "Nobody's ever supposed to swim there, but he liked to."

The day after his death the children and I would look at each other and then turn away. We all tried not to look at Wesley's empty desk. At recess I put it out in the hall so we wouldn't have to see it in the room, empty.

Wesley's mother, pale and shaken, came to school to ask me if the children and I would come to the funeral. She wanted us to sing one of Wesley's favorite songs, one in which he had sung the alto part, true and clear.

Mr. Hart gave his permission, and we went to the funeral together, down the hill to the red brick church. We sang:

Now the day is over,
Night is drawing nigh.
Shadows of the evening
Steal across the sky.

The day after the funeral the children were tense and withdrawn. At recess they stood around in clusters. They didn't want to play baseball or jacks. Inside, they didn't smile when I read to them. They didn't want to play "Simon Says" or have a spelling bee. They were polite and they tried to study, but they were away somewhere.

Finally I decided we had to talk about it. "Let's talk about Wesley."

They looked at me, surprised. After a long moment Stanley said, "I'm going to miss him. He was the best pitcher we had."

"I'm going to miss him, too," I said.

Andy said, "I thought only old people died."

"Our baby died," Ann told us. "They put him in a box. It had pink satin in it. Then they put him in the ground. I didn't like it."

Marvel said, "My mother says when you die you go someplace nice. Not just in a box in the ground, but someplace nice."

Then Boyd, who seldom spoke at all, stood beside his desk. With great dignity he said, "Heaven is a real place. It's real, even if you can't see it."

The children were quiet, but their silence had a new quality. Then Marvel asked, "Like the day of the dust storm, when it got dark? When we couldn't see the sun? You said it was there, even when we couldn't see it. You said we could count on it. Like that? Heaven's like that?"

"Yes, Marvel," I answered. "I think that's what Boyd means."

And for some reason, when Stanley said, "Now let's have arithmetic," we all laughed. Then we went back to work.

CHAPTER
TWENTY • SIX

I spent four years in Riverview. Do we spend our years like money? Do we save bits of their essence for our rainy days? I still draw on my Riverview savings, those scents and sounds of South Dakota.

I can release and savor the aromas of the seasons: fall, and the pungency of red apples and bonfires. Winter, and the sharp spice of evergreen. Spring, with lilacs and apple blossoms.

The sounds are mine, too. May Day, and the muffled, secret laughter of children. Autumn, and the swooshing of roller skates on rough sidewalks. Winter, and the shouts of children as they coast down Schoolhouse Hill on their sleds.

And all those bittersweet years Todd Ashton was there becoming part of my life. Often on Sunday afternoons we'd walk down to the river and sit under the cottonwood trees talking, discovering each other.

"Have you lived in Riverview a long time?" I asked him one day.

"All my life. It's a nice little town. Good people live here. Hard-working, strong people. Real South Dakotans."

He was describing himself, I thought. He would bring me small gifts on ordinary days: a crystal paperweight with a snowstorm inside it; a dragonfly carved from a piece of agate; a piece of softly polished turquoise.

Each of those years, after teaching from September until the end of May, I went home to Vermillion to be with my family and to work on my degree at the University.

Vermillion was incredibly hot, those summers. Often the heels of my white shoes would be coated with black asphalt as the streets melted under the cruel South Dakota sun. Walking the mile to school in the mornings and back again in the heat of the afternoon, I would feel like one of the unredeemed from Dante's *Inferno*, caught forever in some remote fiery circle. At night I would try to sleep, on a cot in the back yard under the box-elder tree. I would study the heavens, looking for a sign. But I never found one.

At home, those summers in Vermillion, everything was difficult. Father was morose and secretive. It was as if we had never talked about the possibilities of change. Mother was controlled but aloof. And Martin became a tall, brooding stranger who retreated from me whenever I approached. He smoldered with something I could not define, something that frightened me.

One afternoon I overheard part of a conversation between Martin and Mother. Martin was saying, "What does it matter, what I do? Nothing ever turns out right anyway."

Mother said, "That's not true. You've got to try, at least."

"Why?" Martin's voice was ugly with anger and something that sounded like hate. "Because you say so?"

"Martin!" Mother's voice was angry, too, but full of pain. Then the door slammed. I wished I had not heard them.

I missed Todd, those summers, but I was afraid to let myself love him. The relationship between my parents stood like a field of ice between me and the possibility of love. For as long as I could remember they had slept in separate rooms. They seemed to move about their lives in a kind of patterned dance, skirting each other, bowing and nodding with courteous formality, but never embracing with intimacy. I thought they must have loved each other in the beginning. But if this was what happened to love, I couldn't trust it.

I went to a church in Vermillion where I was a stranger, where no one knew me, and I talked to the minister. I tried to tell him about the things that were happening: the nebulous fears for my parents, for Martin, for Todd and myself.

He listened attentively. Finally he said, "It seems to me that you are thinking only of yourself in all this. You need to try to help your parents and your brother. Turn out toward others, not inward upon yourself. One finds true satisfaction in self-sacrifice, not in self-indulgence."

But how could I help when I didn't understand what was wrong? After that I felt guilty and immature as well as lonely and confused. I was oppressed, threatened, suffocated by feelings as heavy and humid as the summer itself.

Each fall I would go back to Riverview carrying with me the knowledge of Martin's growing anger, my mother's discontent, and my father's pain. I knew that he was truly in pain. His headaches were frequent and severe. But I also felt sure that he still suffered the old illness of spirit that had always beset him, that he had never been able to conquer. It isolated him from the rest of us, from humanity. I could do nothing to help him; nothing to help any of us. I always left my family with a sense of failure and regret.

And then, one evening early in April, my fourth year in Riverview, my mother telephoned me from Vermillion. I was alarmed because we never spent money on such calls unless there was an emergency.

"What's wrong, Mother?" I was afraid to know.

"Nothing drastic. I don't mean to frighten you. But we've made a sudden decision, and I want you to know about it right away. Your father has to give up his work. The doctor says he must stop now. He's in pain all the time."

She talked rapidly, as if she didn't want me to interrupt her. "I can't face another winter here if I have to do everything again: shoveling snow, the furnace, the house, the shopping. Everything. We're going to move to California where it's warm."

"*California?* Mother, it's so far away."

"I know."

Suddenly I was terrified. "What's wrong with Father? Tell me."

"The pain is coming from a pinched nerve in his spine. They say that nothing can be done for it. His pain will only increase."

My thoughts skittered like dry leaves. "And what about Martin? What about his scholarship to the University?"

"It can't be helped."

"That's awful, Mother. He's been counting on it. He shouldn't have to lose that."

"I know, but it just can't be helped. He can attend a free junior college in Pasadena. We hope you'll come, too. Maybe you could get a scholarship or a loan and finish your degree in California."

But Todd was in Riverview. "When are you going?" I asked my mother.

"As soon as Martin's school is out. An agent is looking for an apartment for us. The bishop is helping us pay for the move."

"I'm sorry about the whole thing," I told my mother. "But I'm not sure that I want to leave Riverview."

Mother's voice sounded forlorn. "Everyone is upset with me, as if it were all my fault. But I have to think about myself, too. I just can't face another winter here."

"I understand. I really do," I told her. "Give my love to Father and Martin. I'll write soon."

Although I resisted leaving Riverview, my life was entwined with theirs and I knew I had to go with them. I was ill at the thought of change, at the thought of leaving Todd, but I was torn. So I told Mr. Hart that I would not be back in the fall. I told Mrs. Larson, too.

"You shouldn't go," she said. "You should stay and marry Todd Ashton. Might as well do it now as later. You're goin' to sometime. I told you that the first day I saw you."

"I have to go," I told her. "My father is sick."

"Well," she said, her scratchy voice full of doom, "that's too bad, but you should stay. Mark my words. Don't say I didn't warn you."

Todd and I walked for a long time, that last night before I left Riverview. The air was fragrant with the spring scents I loved, but lilac was the fragrance of melancholy. When Todd held me, kissing me good-night, I clung to him as if it were for the last time. For all I knew, it was.

But he seemed cheerful when he said, "I'll take you and your trunk to the station in the morning. Nine o'clock?"

"Yes. I'm checking the trunk through to Pasadena. I won't need it in Denver."

He brushed the hair back from my forehead in that way he had. "What are you going to do in Denver, anyway?"

"I'm going to sit in a hotel room and think. And I'm going to hear Richard Tucker sing. I have my ticket to his concert."

"I don't even know who he is," Todd said. "But I'll learn. We can hear music together."

I stared at him.

"I'll be along." He smiled. "Maybe in the fall. I think it would be interesting to live in California for a while."

"You do?" I couldn't believe he really meant it, even while I hoped it might be true.

In the morning, at the train station I thought, *I may never see him again.* How could I count on anything as far away as California, as far away as fall? And besides, I was still afraid to commit myself to him.

When the train pulled away and I heard the lonely, climbing whistle, I felt that part of my life had died. Sitting there alone, speeding away from the children I had come to love, from Riverview, from Todd, I didn't dare to hope that I might be traveling not only away from a safe, familiar place, but toward a new vista, mysterious and bright.

I tried to hide my face so that no one could see my misery. And as I looked out the window at the spring fields, the flowering trees, I saw them for the last time through tears.

CHAPTER
TWENTY • SEVEN

W hen the train pulled into the Denver station I took a cab to the hotel where I had written for a room. The clerk was polite but regretful. "I'm very sorry," he said, "but we have no record of your reservation. It seems your letter never reached us. We're full because we're hosting a convention. I'm afraid every hotel in town is full." He must have seen the desperation in my eyes because he said, "I'll see what I can do for you. Why don't you go have some lunch while I make a few calls?"

I wasn't hungry, but I knew I should eat something, so I had tea and cinnamon toast. When I went back to the desk, the clerk was smiling.

"I hope you'll approve of this," he said. "I've found a room for you in a convent." I must have looked surprised because he added, "Temporarily, of course. The sisters will be glad to have you. And we'd like to pay your cab fare. We feel responsible, in a way."

Something about his concern and generosity made me feel safe. Even the cab driver seemed fatherly. As he let me out in front of the convent he asked, "Got everything, have you? Don't leave anything in the cab. You'll be fine here; better than at the hotel. Now you take care."

When I knocked at the door of the convent a smiling nun opened it and indicated silently that I was to follow her. She led me toward a room at the end of a long hall. She knocked and then opened the door, motioning for me to go in.

The woman who greeted me was regal. Her beautiful, classic face was serene, her voice gentle and musical. "I am Sister Benedicta," she said. "You are welcome here with us." We talked about small matters, but I was so enchanted with her that I heard only her voice, not what she said.

Finally, though, she said, "Before I show you to your room I'd like to tell you a bit about our customs. We ask you to cover your head while you are in our house." She handed me a small lace cap and a hair pin. "Dinner is at six in the refectory. Our breakfast at seven is a silent meal. Luncheon is at noon. I'll show you the library and garden. You may do whatever you like. We'll be happy to have you join us in the chapel for services if you wish to."

"I'd like to ask one more thing," I said. "I have a ticket for Richard Tucker's concert tonight. May I call a cab from here?"

She seemed delighted. "Perhaps you would like to ride with us. Several of us are going." Seeing that I was confused, she smiled and said, "We are not entirely divorced from the world, you know. I am a musician, too, and I teach musicians."

So I went to the concert with several of the sisters. They sat downstairs, I in the balcony. We arranged to meet in the foyer after the concert. The building was cavernous, the stage vast, and I seemed very far away from it. The piano, standing there alone, was almost lost.

The singer entered to the applause of the audience. I studied him through my binoculars. He looked very serious in his black dress suit. I was not prepared for the torrent of sound that poured from his throat, filling that huge hall with lustrous, vital tone.

That was the first time I heard the great tenor aria from Mendelssohn's *Elijah*: "If with all your hearts ye truly seek me, Ye shall ever truly find me. Thus saith our God." I felt as if he were singing directly to me.

That night I fell asleep feeling cherished and safe. The next day I moved in a charm, surrounded by peace. In the evening I went to Vespers in the chapel and I heard the pure, sweet voices sing plainsong, the long, flowing phrases weaving in and out of the candlelight in medieval ambience.

The next morning I talked with Sister Benedicta. I entrusted her with all my fears: the fears for my parents and Martin, for myself and Todd. And I shared with her my feelings of guilt.

When I had told her what the minister in Vermillion had said, she looked troubled. "I agree, of course, that it is important to think of others, to serve and to help. But before one can do that one must be at peace with oneself. My dear Julie, although we have only just met, I feel that I know you well. You remind me of another young woman who was troubled and distressed. And impatient."

"You, Sister?"

"Yes. But I believe the answer that was given to me is probably not the answer for you. You will be led to your own answer. I see you as a person with a large capacity for loving. You must not be afraid to give and receive love. Your Todd sounds like a fine young man. I can see you as wife and mother, as a useful, vital woman moving in the world with confidence and strength.

"Your parents? I have no way of knowing what troubles them. The reasons must be deep, and perhaps you cannot fathom them. But one day you may. I feel sure that they need you near them now.

"And your brother. I see how much you care for him, how much you are troubled that he removes himself from you just now. Even though he seems far away at this present time, one day he may return. When he, himself, is happier, perhaps. And if he does not, you must love him anyway."

Her voice was so kind, her eyes so loving and wise, that I began to cry. I cried for a long time in that quiet room. When I was calm again she walked to the door with me, and out to the cab that waited to take me to the train station. She kissed me first on one cheek and then on the other. Her lips were cool and light as the wings of a white moth. Then she made the sign of the cross over me with a wide, sweeping motion. She walked away from me. I watched until the convent door closed behind her.

CHAPTER
TWENTY · EIGHT

❦

The year of Pearl Harbor I was teaching a fourth-grade class in Long Beach, California. Long Beach is a navy town, and we had many navy children in our school. Nine-year-old Lucy and her brother lost their father at Pearl Harbor.

"Why do we have to have wars, anyway?" one of the boys asked, soon after that.

I fielded the question. "What do you think causes them?"

Bruce, mature beyond his years, said, "Because somebody always wants what somebody else has. If they can't get it by asking, they'll try to take it. That makes wars."

Mariko and Hiroko Hinobi, our twins, were unusually quiet, and as the weeks passed they became even more so. They studied and did all their work, everything they were supposed to do. But they didn't smile much anymore. The words *treachery* and *barbarism* were in the air, but they didn't apply to anyone I knew. I thought of my father, long ago, in another war.

Todd had followed me to California, just as he'd said he would. We knew he would soon be drafted into the service. Martin had already enlisted and was gone, we didn't know where.

The thought of war, the urgencies that war produces, brought Todd and me to a decision. We made plans to marry as soon as school was out in the spring. We had waited long enough. Too long. We sensed that our life together could be brief, that we might be separated for months, at the very least. So, like many other young people, we planned in spite of everything.

On my way home from school one day in March I stopped, as I often did, at Mr. Hinobi's little flower shop. A display of white chrysanthemums stood in the window.

"Good day, Miss Teacher," Mr. Hinobi said with that slight inclination of the head that implied the most exquisite courtesy. "The chrysanthemums? I believe you like them especially?"

"Yes. They are beautiful. May I have three, please?"

He chose three perfect flowers and added some greens. He wrapped them in a cone of white paper and handed them to me. I touched a rich petal. "I hope there will be some of these in June," I told him. "I'd like some at my wedding."

"Ah, so you marry? What happy news."

"Yes. When school is out. I hope you will help me with my flowers."

He bowed to me. "We will wish for you great happiness. Do you marry a military person?"

"He isn't yet. But I expect he soon will be in the army. My brother is, already."

"Yes." He looked grave. "Yes. War is a great separator, is it not? And there is no joy in it for anyone. Not for anyone."

"I know."

"My daughters," he said, "do they study well?"

"Yes. Always. They are lovely children, Mr. Hinobi. You and your wife must be very proud of them."

"Thank you, Miss Teacher. We are happy to have them in your class. It is a fine school we have."

I thought of that conversation one spring morning when the telephone in my schoolroom rang and it was my principal. "Please send Mariko and Hiroko to the office right away."

144

Troubled, I turned away from the phone and looked at them. Silently, without waiting for me to speak, they stacked their few belongings on top of their desks: pencil boxes, notebooks, the pictures they had painted that morning. They stood, picked up their things, and came to the front of the room. Mariko handed me her painting, a yellow chrysanthemum. Hiroko gave me a note. They bowed solemnly to me, to the children, to the flag in its holder beside the blackboard. Then they walked out of the room.

I read the note. It was written on white rice paper, thin and fragile.

Dear Miss Teacher,

My wife and I wish to thank you for the skill and patience you have shown in the teaching of our daughters, and for the affection you have given them. They return that affection. May the time come soon when we will once again join each other in respect and friendship. We will think of you while we are away.

> *Yours with sincerity,*
> *Tokashi Hinobi*

That afternoon at recess the children and I stood at the edge of the school yard where it bordered Atlantic Boulevard. We watched military trucks go by, loaded with Japanese families. It was quiet there beside the street. We didn't hear any voices. No one called out. No babies cried.

We heard the bell ring inside the school, signaling us to go in. But we didn't leave. Finally we saw the truck carrying Mariko and Hiroko and their parents away from us. As they went by, the twins waved to us with the small American flags they held.

While I watched, the colors of those flags melted into each other. The stars blurred. The trucks moved slowly along the boulevard. We couldn't even see the last of them, the convoy was so long. After a while the children and I went back to our room together.

CHAPTER
TWENTY · NINE

I went home for the Christmas vacation and found my father dying. When I stepped into my parents' house late that afternoon my mother greeted me. She was thin and pale and there were purple smudges under her eyes. Even then I was aware of her control, of the discipline she always imposed upon herself.

"Mother, what's wrong?" I asked her.

"It's your father," she said quietly. "He's very sick."

Then I noticed the odor that permeated the house: a powerful odor, sickeningly sweet. And I knew what was wrong with my father.

"Why didn't you let me know?" I asked her. "I'd have come home. How long has he been like this? You should have let me know."

"It's been progressing for weeks. The doctor says there is nothing to be done. He couldn't survive an operation, not with his weakened heart. We didn't want to call you away from your work." She lit a piece of string that lay in a shallow pan. "This helps with the odor." She went to the kitchen, and I followed her. "It's time for his medication. I'll give it to him and then you can go in."

I took my suitcase into my room, hung up my clothes, and combed my hair. Then I went toward my father's room.

"Go on in," my mother said. "Don't be surprised if he doesn't know you. He gets confused. I'm not sure he realizes how sick he is."

I went into my father's room. He lay with his eyes closed, his glasses on the table beside him. There was no book on the table. I knew then that he did know how sick he was. I looked down at him wondering how my mother had borne this alone, and how I would be able to stand it now. He opened his eyes.

"Hello, Father."

He looked at me silently. Then he pointed to his glasses. I slipped them on for him. He looked up at me, but still he didn't speak.

"Father, don't you know me?"

Then he smiled and said, "Did you think I would not know my own daughter? My Julie?"

I sighed with relief that he knew me. Helping him take off his glasses, I laid them down again and then sat beside him and took his hand.

"I'm glad you have come," he said.

"I'd have come sooner if I'd known." He nodded and then almost at once he was asleep again. I went to the kitchen where my mother was working. "You should have let me know sooner. I really wish you had."

"But there was nothing you could have done. Nothing."

I could have been here, Mother, I thought. I could have been a part of my father's death that much sooner. I could have helped you bear it. I could have tried, as I always used to, to understand you.

All through my childhood I knew there was something different about my parents. They were courteous to each other, but I had seldom seen them touch each other. I had never seen them kiss, although they were loving, sometimes, with me and with Martin.

I would watch the parents of my friends when I was in their homes. I would see them happy with each other, friendly, touching, and I would think there must be a way to help my mother and father be like this, a magic formula. But I never discovered it.

"Father," I would ask, as a child, "are you and Mother mad at each other?"

"No. No," he would say. "It is just that we are both quiet people. We are not angry."

"Tell me again about your first wife," I would beg him, "the one who died." This seemed mysterious to me. "Please tell me about her."

And he would say, "She was very young when she died. I have told you. Her name was Elsa."

"Mother," I would ask, when we were alone, "do you love Father?"

She would look embarrassed and say, "Why, Julie, how can you ask me that?" Then she would change the subject. But she never gave me a real answer. Now I realized that.

After supper, when we had prepared my father for the night I said, "You go to bed now, Mother. I'll stay up with him. You can show me what to do."

She did not protest. She showed me the medications and then she went to her room. I wondered how long it had been since she had really slept. I went in to tell her goodnight.

"Call if you need me for anything," she said. "Promise you'll call me if he gets bad."

"I will, Mother. Sleep well."

Settling myself in the big chair in my father's room, I watched him, dozed, and watched again. In the distance I heard carolers. "God rest you merry, Gentlemen," they sang. And I thought, *God rest you. God rest you easy, Father.*

Toward midnight he woke and I gave him his medicine. His skin was waxen, his breathing shallow. The strong, sweet odor of his dying filled the room.

"Did you know," my father began, "did I ever tell you about my wife? about Elsa?"

"Yes, Father." I had been fascinated, as a child, by the knowledge that my father had been married before. I often

149

wondered how my mother felt about that. They never talked about it together, as far as I knew, and my mother mentioned it only rarely.

"Did I tell you how she died, my young Elsa?"

"No, not that, Father. Only that you had been married just a year." I took his hand. "Do you think you can sleep now?"

"I must tell you how she died. Your mother knows but I think she has never told you. I must tell you." But he drifted off to sleep again. I thought about the two young people who had come from Germany and bought a ranch in Wyoming to make their way in a new land.

A little later my father began to speak again as if there had been no pause. "It is a blizzard. A terrible storm. Never have I seen such a storm. Elsa is in labor. There is no way to get a doctor. No way to get any help." His eyes were wide. His voice shook, and his German accent thickened as it did when he was excited.

"I am alone with her, and there is only the wind and the cold. The snow is blowing. Elsa is in labor, in hard labor. *Ach*, she suffers, and I can do nothing."

"Father, that was a long time ago. You did all you could."

But now he was weeping, and he spoke as if I had not interrupted him. "She cries out. She screams. *Ach*, I love her so, and I can do nothing. *Nichts. Nichts.*" His hands pulled at the sheets.

I wiped his forehead with a damp cloth and offered him some water, but he didn't notice.

"All the night she labors. In the morning our son is born, and he is dead. Our baby son, he is never breathing. My Elsa, she is never breathing anymore. *Mein Gott. Mein lieber Gott.*"

I wiped away the tears that ran down his cheeks and over his lips. Why had they never told me this story?

Maybe I could have understood some of it while I was growing up. I could have understood the pain.

And still he talked. "For how many days I am alone with them I do not know. I lose the count. Until men come to dig us out of the snow. They see my dead Elsa and our dead son. I have put him in her arms. Those men, they cry with me. We cry together. Grown men. Strangers." Finally, exhausted, he slept.

I felt a rush of love for my father. A rush of pity and love for all of them: my father and mother and Elsa, the young German girl who might have been my mother, for the baby who never had a chance to be my brother.

Then my father spoke again. "Julie, is it nearly Christmas?"

"Just a few more days," I told him.

"Please sing for me. *Stille Nacht.*"

So I sang *Silent Night* as he loved it, in German, knowing that I might never be able to sing it or hear it again without grief. I sang it that night for my father. He reached for my hand and fell asleep holding it.

Later he woke again. "Julie," he began, his thin fingers plucking at the sheets.

"Yes, Father?"

"I have thought to tell you this long before now. It was not your mother's fault."

"What do you mean?"

"Our marriage. That it was troubled. It was not your mother's fault."

"Father," I began, but I did not really know what to say.

"When I meet your mother I am already beginning to be old. At forty I am already old. But your mother and I, we think to make a home together. We are both lonely. There was love between us. I am sure there was love."

"Yes, Father, I'm sure, too."

He drew a deep, shuddering breath.

"Are you in pain?"

"*Ja*, there is pain. Still, there is pain. But nothing to be cured with medicine." Then, after a pause, without bitterness or judgment he said, "Your mother is afraid. She is afraid of love. Always, always afraid. I cannot help her. I try often, but I do not know how."

I thought he was finally asleep but he spoke again, almost whispering. "Always I would see my Elsa. In my mind I would see Elsa. I would see her laughing. I would see her dead. But always, Elsa. It was not your mother's fault."

"It's not anybody's fault," I told him just before he slept again. If I had known. If I had only known. Why must understanding come so late? Perhaps it is true that each child puts his universe together with small pieces, like a jigsaw puzzle, one part at a time. And only much later, with widened vision, the adult sees the whole picture come clear.

In the morning my mother came in and woke me. We had our breakfast together. "Did you sleep at all?" she asked me. "You would have called me, wouldn't you?"

"I didn't need you," I assured her. "I'm glad you slept."

All that day Mother and I were in and out of my father's room, restless with waiting. He slept, not responding to anything. The doctor came by in the afternoon. "He may not wake again," he told us. "I think it will be soon."

Martin should be here, too, I thought. *Someday he may wish he had been here, too.*

And I wished Todd could be with us, but he was at work. I longed to be with him. Our love was strong, and I knew at last that I was freed from the fear that we would be like my parents. I wanted to rush to him, to hold him, to hurry the date of our marriage. To be with him completely.

After supper that evening Mother and I went into Father's room to watch and wait together. I heard the carolers again, and it was hard to believe that Christmas was on its way toward us in spite of everything.

My mother spoke softly as she leaned to straighten the covers around Father's shoulders. "I wish I could have shown him. I was never able to show him how much I love him." She twisted her wedding band as she talked.

"Things were so different when I was young. My parents were strict. Cold and strict. My mother never talked to me. Not about important things. I was ignorant. No woman should grow up as ignorant as I." She paused. "I waited until so late to marry. I was afraid . . ."

Then, just as I thought she had finished speaking she added softly, "I think he always wished that I were someone else."

"Oh Mother," I began.

But she broke in. "It's true. He wished that I were someone else."

We sat there watching my father sleep away the rest of his life. The pauses in his breathing became longer. We could barely see the covers rise and fall.

At about midnight my mother said, "He's gone." She touched his hand, his face, and said again, "He's gone."

She called first the doctor and then the mortuary. The men came quickly. Going into the bedroom they put my father's body on a stretcher and they walked out of the house carefully, as if to protect him from something.

When they had gone I made tea, and my mother and I sat together in the kitchen, in the dim, cold light, until dawn.

CHAPTER
T H I R T Y

❦

When the war ended Todd and I had been apart for thirty-five months. It might as well have been thirty-five years. I have never been able to fathom the intricacies of Einstein's theory, but even I know that all things are relative. Days when the mail came through from Europe were shorter than days when it did not. The December of the Battle of the Bulge, when there was no mail at all, lasted forever. Nights were longer than days.

And then, eons later, one September evening in California, the telephone rang and it was Todd calling from New Jersey.

"I'm coming home," he said. "They're sending us on army planes, and I should be there in a couple of days."

I couldn't say anything. I tried, but no words would come.

"Darling, did you hear me?" He laughed. "I'm coming home."

His deep voice was warm and familiar. The sound of it unlocked my silence and I said, "I wish you were here now. Are you all right? You sound wonderful."

When we finally broke the connection, the silence between California and New Jersey was alive.

The next day while my mother and I cleaned the house we had shared for nearly three years, I watched for Todd. Although he had said, "a couple of days," all morning I listened for him. I ran each time the phone rang. I went to the window every fifteen minutes.

Listening to the midday news on the radio, my mother and I heard the announcer say, "An army plane has crashed over Texas, killing everyone on board. The plane was loaded with servicemen returning to the West Coast from a base in New Jersey. Names are being withheld pending notification of next of kin."

Mother and I looked at each other. My mouth was dry, my hands and feet numb. Then my legs began to shake and I sat down. Soon it seemed imperative that I do something. If I acted, if I took a positive step, perhaps everything would be all right. So I telephoned the Red Cross. They had heard about the crash, but they had no information. Yes, they would take my number and call when they had further news.

I went next door to tell my neighbor. Mac was a newspaper reporter. Maybe he could find out something. Sharon sat me down and brought coffee that I couldn't drink. She called Mac at the paper. Yes, he would try to get some information.

I went home to wait. I tried to pray. *Oh God, Oh God,* I said over and over. *Oh God, please.* That day went on for years. Finally it was dark. My mother thought we should try to eat something. We were in the kitchen when the doorbell rang.

My heart really did stop beating for a moment then. I put the palms of my hands against the tile of the sink. It felt cool. Mother went to the door. I could visualize the Western Union messenger. He would be young and in a hurry.

Mother came to me then, in the kitchen, and she didn't speak. She only looked at me. I could tell nothing from her expression. She nodded toward the hall. I walked the miles to the living room.

And then I saw Todd. Somehow I was in his arms, his body solid and real against my own, his shoulders firm and strong under my hands.

Afterward he said he hadn't been able to understand why my mother opened the door, stared at him, let him in, and walked away from him without a word. Or why I held him for so long without speaking, desperately, with something beyond welcome.

Our "happily ever after" began then, but it was touched with a feeling of grief and guilt that I have never lost. My husband came back to me safely. But what of those other families whose men did not come home that night? The whole war. To survive it all, to be so close to home, and then . . .

I am sure of one thing. God does not ask us to earn or deserve our lives. Life is a gift.

CHAPTER
THIRTY • ONE

❦

*An ordinary seeing of dreams is common to all men,
and arises in our fancies in different modes and
forms. . . . Thus, the thirsty man, dreaming, seems to
be among springs, the man who is in need of food
seems to be at a feast . . . the nutritive part of the soul
is operative during sleep, and some echoes and
shadows of those things which happen in our waking
moments . . . are pictured; some echo of memory still
lingering in this division of the soul.*
Gregory of Nyssa
On the Making of Man

When I was waiting the birth of our first child I took long afternoon naps. A wisteria vine cascaded outside my window. The scent of delicate lavender blossoms, the contented sound of bees were part of my sleeping and my waking. My own sense of well-being was enormous.

The Fourth of July birth was rather like the holiday on which Meg arrived: splendid and spectacular. My labor was strong and rapid, and delivery appeared to be imminent before the doctor was ready. There was no time for a general anesthetic, so I was given occasional deep breaths of gas between the efforts that are termed so perfectly *labor*.

I knew I was laboring well. I was participating in a unique event and I tried to obey the doctor's instructions.

"Now. Push. That's good. Again. Push."

The pain was huge, all-enveloping. And between pains came the deep, refreshing breaths of gas that induced dreams.

I floated in space. Meteors flashed by, glowing like lamps. Planets with multiple moons rolled past. I was in the midst of the first day, before there was order. But I was neither lonely nor afraid.

A voice called to me. It was wordless, as clear and direct as a Bach trumpet.

I tried to answer. "Is someone there?"

No answering words. Only the silver trumpet.

Then, after eons, caught in the grip of gigantic, unendurable pain, I heard the voice again. Rising out of swirling space, it swelled in one long, perfect tone, the essence of music. I heard it.

The pain stopped, the light faded, the voice of the trumpet ceased and a mortal voice said, "You have a daughter, and she's perfect."

Someone laid Meg on my chest and I saw her. Her eyes looked straight into my own, and we knew each other. We had known each other from the Beginning.

Two years later Alice was born. Quickly, quietly, easily. No dreams attended this birth. They came later.

One night when she was about six I dreamed that Alice and I were sitting on a sled at the top of a formidable snow-covered mountain. She sat ahead of me and my arms were around her. Unseen hands pushed, and we started a long ride down the steep, cold slope. I knew that at some point, around one of the twisting curves, hidden in clouds, I would have to release Alice. She would continue the long, dangerous journey alone.

At breakfast the next morning fragments of the dream clung to me and I was oppressed and disturbed. Alice said, "I had a funny dream last night."

Almost knowing what she was going to say, I asked, "What did you dream?"

"You and I were on a sled at the top of a mountain. Somebody pushed and we went flying down. You hung on to me, so I wasn't scared. But I kept thinking, *What if she lets go?*"

I stared at her. Then I asked, "Did I let go?"

"I don't know." Alice buttered a piece of toast. "I woke up."

Later that year there was a second shared dream, and the mystery of it remains with me still.

Todd and I had given up hoping for another child, but in that year I found myself to be pregnant. I was ill most of the time, and we decided to wait to tell the girls. But I saw, in my mind, our family as a unit of five.

At the end of the third month we told Meg and Alice. They were jubilant. Over and over again they wanted to hear about their own births. Over and over I told them. We got out the baby things, and the girls marveled at their delicacy, wondering if anyone could really be small enough to wear them.

And then one midnight came the emergency: the frantic call to our neighbor to come stay with the sleeping girls, the drive along dark streets to the hospital, the rushing blood.

Later there was the drive home again, the empty aching body, the unfulfilled promise.

The girls were desolate and full of questions.

Why did it happen?	*I don't know.*
Did it hurt?	*Yes.*
Was it a boy or a girl?	*We don't know.*
Will we ever have a baby?	*No. Not now.*
Will I have a baby someday?	*I hope so.*
Will I?	*I hope so.*
But why did it happen?	*I don't know.*
Are you and Daddy sad?	*Yes.*

Then one morning, months later, Alice said to me, "I dreamed about our baby."

"What did you dream?" I knew. I knew.

"He was in a sort of forest. I saw his back. There was a swing. I think he was happy."

I had dreamed, too. I walked in a forest. The trees were dense, the leaves dappled with sun. Ahead of me in the distance was a swing, suspended from one of the trees. A child was swinging in it silently, gently. I could see the curve of his back.

I walked down the aisle of trees toward the child in the swing, but before I reached it the swing was empty. It was still in motion, but it was empty. I felt that someone waited in the forest. It was like the landscape of my lost, childhood island. An echo from Eden.

Alice and I looked at each other. Her eyes were wide and solemn. "We both dreamed it, didn't we? Like that other time?"

"Yes."

"I don't understand it," she said.

"I know. I don't understand it, either. But I'm glad it happened."

"Me, too," Alice said. Then she added, as if she were telling me a secret, "I think the place in our dream was real."

"I think so, too," I said.

CHAPTER
THIRTY · TWO

The house on Laurel Street was just the right size for the four of us: Todd and me, Meg and Alice. It was fairly new when we bought it, but ivy geraniums and roses already bordered the front walk and the property line in back. Although a few young trees had begun to give shade, we planned to plant several more against the strong California sun.

Todd built a playhouse out in back for the girls and soon the neighborhood children were enjoying it with Meg and Alice.

One day our next-door neighbor, Nan, said, "Watch out for Ron and Myron. They live in the house across the street."

"What do you mean, 'Watch out'?"

"Just be careful. They nearly got Sue one time."

Sue was the age of Alice. "They nearly got her?" The words sounded ominous. "What do you mean?" I repeated.

"They're bullies. Especially the older one. They're just what you'd expect from a place like that." Nan sounded scornful.

We had been concerned about that property when we moved in. The house looked uncared for, the paint dirty. Two broken windows were stuffed with papers. Weeds had taken over the yard. Piles of trash lay in heaps around the house. I found myself wishing I couldn't see it from my window and somehow the thought made me feel guilty.

One day seven-year-old Alice ran crying into the house, nine-year-old Meg following. "There are two bad boys out there. They won't go home."

I went out. The boys appeared to be about the ages of my daughters. They looked like any other boys: blue jeans, sneakers, tousled hair. Methodically, the older boy was breaking the toy dishes while the younger one dumped sand on the floor.

"Hey boys," I said, "that's not the way to play in here."

Neither boy paid any attention. I took the arm of the one who was breaking the dishes. "Stop that," I ordered.

He shook me off. "Make me." The look in his eyes was ugly.

The younger boy tossed a handful of sand in my face. Half-blinded and furious I tried to get it out of my eyes. I lurched toward them screaming, "You come here," as they ran off.

After the boys had gone I thought, *I should have tried to talk to them. I got angry too quickly. Maybe if I get to know them better, I can reason with them.*

That night after the girls were in bed I talked to Todd about it. "What do you think we should do? I've never seen anything like them. Like the way they act, I mean."

"Maybe they were just having a bad day," Todd said. "Why don't you give it another try? Have the girls give them a special invitation. Maybe they feel left out."

But Meg balked at that the next day. "I don't want to."

"Maybe if you and Alice are nice to them, they'll be nice to you. Let's try it. All right?"

We tried it and it was a disaster. Ron and Myron threw the food, dumped sand, and stomped the dolls.

Alice wailed. "They broke Annie." No doll could ever replace Annie.

"Todd," I told him that night, "we've got to do something. They're fiends."

"I'll go over." Todd said. "We'd better try to stop it now before anything really gets started."

He wasn't gone long, and before he had time to tell me about his encounter with the Kilbers, the boys began to scream. We were sure we could hear blows falling, even from that distance. It went on for a long time.

"Todd, make him stop."

"He's an animal," Todd said, angry. I'd never seen him so angry. "He stood there with his can of beer and said he'd fix the little devils so they'd never do *that* again." Todd sighed. "Well, maybe he has fixed it."

But of course he hadn't. We never knew what it was going to be. They'd sneak over and throw mud on our clean windows. They dumped a load of garbage on our porch. They broke the toys and cornered the girls, hitting them whenever they could.

One day, though, Myron came over while I was weeding the roses. He was the little one. "What are you doing?" He crouched to look.

"Weeding."

He watched for a while. "Those flowers sure are pretty." He touched a rose.

"Where's Ron?" I asked.

"He can't come out. He's tied to the bed."

"Tied to the bed? What for?"

"He started a fire on the living-room floor," Myron told me. "I don't know why Mom got so mad. It was just a little fire. But she says he has to stay tied up till Dad gets home, even if he has to wet the bed. Then he'll get it for that, too. I'm glad I'm not him."

"I'm sorry," I said. What was I sorry for? I suppose, that I knew I couldn't stop what was coming for Ron.

"We're going to have a baby," Myron said. "Mom's mad. She yelled at Dad and said it was all his fault. Then he yelled at her." He poked at the dirt. "Everybody's mad."

In a moment he said, "I wish I had some flowers."

"What for?"

"To give my mom so she wouldn't be mad anymore." Then he added, almost shyly, "I'm sorry I was mean to Alice."

I cut some roses for him, snipping off the thorns. He dashed off and disappeared into his house.

That night the girls were asleep and Todd was out on a business appointment when I heard screams again. They rose higher and higher until I could not stand hearing them. Before I was conscious of making a decision, I was beating on the Kilbers' door.

The man came, naked from the waist up, his broad chest matted and gleaming with sweat, a leather belt in his hand. I saw, looking past him, the woman sitting in a chair, and my roses in a milk bottle on the table.

"What do *you* want?"

"Stop beating that boy," I heard myself say. "You have to stop it."

"Mind your own business, lady." He shut the door.

The screams started again. I went home and rushed to the bathroom. I began vomiting. I retched until I was weak, until the screams had stopped.

✳ ✳ ✳

When Meg came home from school the next day she told me, "Ron got sick in school today and they took him to the nurse."

"Then what happened?" I asked her.

"At recess he grabbed me and said, 'I'll kill you if you tell.' I don't know what he meant. Anyway, I told him I won't tell."

"I won't either," Alice said.

"Don't worry about it," I told them. But I worried about it. I went over and knocked on the door. Mrs. Kilber came.

"Hi," she said. "Come on in. Sit down, if you can find a place. I don't feel much like fixing things up." Before I could say anything she went on. "Thanks for the flowers. I love roses, but we don't have time to keep a garden."

"I've come to talk about Ron," I told her. "I don't know what to do."

"I don't know what to do, either. He's so mean, and he makes Myron do mean things and then Les beats them both. They just get worse. Myron used to be so sweet. He still is, sometimes.

"I tell Les there has to be a better way. But he just says that's the way his dad did to him, and what's good enough for him is good enough for his kids. And now I suppose we'll have another boy and the whole thing will start over again."

"Maybe it will be a girl," I said, knowing even as I spoke how silly it was. That couldn't make any difference. "Anyway, Mrs. Kilber, Ron has to leave Meg alone. I won't have him scaring her like that."

"Why don't you call me Vi?"

I wouldn't let her change the subject. "About Ron," I said firmly. "Tell him to leave Meg alone."

"I'll try," she said, her voice hopeless. "Sometimes boys tease girls because they like them."

"This isn't like that. Meg is really afraid of him. All the children are afraid of him."

"I'll talk to him. Maybe he'll listen to me this time."

But he must not have listened because one day soon after that Alice came running into the house to get me. I followed her out to the playhouse. The boys had Meg on the floor and she was struggling. Leaning over them I said to Alice, "Run get Nan. Quick." Then I saw that the boys were trying to force Meg to eat dirt.

"Eat it. Eat it," Ron screamed at her. "Eat it. If you eat enough, maybe you won't talk about me anymore."

Soon Nan and I had Meg free. Nan took my weeping daughters into the house and I, holding both boys in a grip that would surely leave bruises, took them home. They kicked and yelled, but I was so angry that I found strength I didn't know I had.

"Vi," I called at her door. "Vi, come here."

"What is it now?" She stood in the doorway in a soiled shift, her hair stringy, her dirty feet bare.

"If you don't do something about these filthy boys, I will," I stormed at her, out of my mind with rage and fear and frustration. "I've had all I'm going to take. We'll sign a complaint against you, all of us. The whole neighborhood. We've had enough."

"Oh, God, don't do that," she said, pushing at the boys. "They take your kids away if they get complaints. They put them somewhere. They'll be better. I'll make them be better. They'll be good. Don't do that."

I walked away from that house trembling. I walked away from its peeling paint, its broken windows and its foul smell. I walked away from all of it, knowing that there would be more screaming. *Isn't there any other way?* I asked myself. *Isn't there anything we can do to help those boys?*

※ ※ ※

That night when the screams began Todd called the police and asked that an officer come to talk to us when they had finished at Kilbers'.

When the two policemen came to our house Todd told them, "We feel we really must do something about this. Things get worse. We don't like to have trouble in the neighborhood, but we keep thinking about what will finally happen to those boys."

One of the men handed Todd a form. "The only way we can do anything is to have you sign this complaint," he said. "Until we get a signed complaint all we can do is warn them. And that hasn't been doing any good." He shook his head. "You think you can get used to anything in this kind of work. But I never do get used to the way some people treat their children."

So we signed a formal complaint against our neighbors. We wrote out the whole dismal story and said yes, we'd go to court if we had to.

After that Les didn't beat the boys. At least, we didn't hear them screaming. But one day when I was working in the back yard Myron came over.

"Ron dropped Dad's watch down the toilet," he told me. "Dad says he's going to kill him. He put him in the trunk of our car and drove away. Mom's scared."

Just then Vi called Myron home. I went with him. "Is it true?" I asked her. "Myron says Les has taken Ron away. Where has he taken him?"

"God knows." Her voice sounded dull.

About an hour later Les drove up and parked the car in the driveway. I watched from my window. I saw him go into the house alone. When he had gone I went to stand by the trunk of the car, not caring who saw me. I heard whimpering sounds coming from inside. *Dear God, the memories this child will have,* I thought, as I went into my house to call the police. I told them what had happened, and I could not keep my voice steady as I talked.

Soon they arrived. They got Les and I watched them unlock the trunk. One of the policemen carried Ron into the house. They were in there a long time and when they came out, Les was with them. Then it was very quiet.

After a while I went over. Vi was sitting on a kitchen chair. She wasn't crying. She was just sitting there. "They say they might not keep Les very long," she told me, "but this time it's different. I don't know what's going to happen. Ron's asleep."

"I'm so sorry, Vi." *I've helped bring you to this,* I thought, *and all I can say is that I'm sorry.*

"They said maybe they'll have to take the kids away from us. But maybe we can get one more chance. It all depends." Then she looked straight at me and said, "I told Les no matter what happens I'll leave him if he ever hurts the boys again. I mean it. I'll leave him."

"I hope you won't have to," I told her, unable to imagine how she could possibly do anything else.

"I don't know what I'd do," she said, her hand against her swollen belly, "but if he ever touches them again, I'll go and take them with me. Maybe my folks would take us in, the boys and me."

Les was not gone long. The next day I saw him sitting on the porch step. A radio blared. He tossed beer cans into the yard as he finished with them. They piled up beside the step.

About a week later Myron came over while I was washing windows. "My dad's mad at you."

"He is?" I polished a pane of glass.

"He cussed about you."

"Oh?" Uneasily I washed another pane.

"He says he's going to fix you." Before I could think of anything to say he went on. "My mom's going to the hospital pretty soon. Maybe tonight. She's got a bad stomach ache. That means she's going to have the baby."

"Who's going to take care of you?"

"Nobody. Just my dad."

Late in the afternoon I saw Les drive off with Vi. I heard the boys laughing and yelling. They ran out and turned on the hose, soaking each other. They aimed the water in the open window. After a while they went back in and I heard the television.

I took them some cold chicken and potato salad at supper time, half ashamed that I didn't ask them to eat with us.

Todd went out on business. I was still reading, much later, when I heard someone on the porch. It was Les, and he was drunk. He rattled the door, but the hook held. I stood there looking at him, only a flimsy screen door between us.

"Well hello, neighbor." His speech was thick. "Come on out and drink to my new kid. It's a boy."

"I'd better not." I tried not to sound afraid. "Why don't you go home? Your boys are alone."

"Why don't you go home?" His voice mimicked mine. He pulled at the door, shaking it, kicking it. "Bitch," he snarled. "Meddling bitch." The venom in his voice was chilling. Suddenly the hook gave and Les was standing there, his face close to mine. He grabbed my chin in his huge hand.

"I told you once to mind your own business." His voice was cold and he tried to speak distinctly. "You called the cops."

He tightened his grip on my chin. I felt my mouth pucker into an obscene shape. My teeth jammed against the inner flesh of my cheeks.

"Call them again. Just once. Call them again. Maybe you want something real nice to happen to your precious girls. Those stuck-up, prissy kids. Call the cops, Honey. Just call them."

With a push he let me go. I staggered back, and he turned and lurched across the street. I locked the door and bolted it. Then I went in to look at Meg and Alice, sleeping and safe. I touched each girl and I started to tremble. I was still shaking when Todd came home.

"What's wrong?" he asked me. "Has something happened?"

"Oh Todd, he's going to hurt the girls. He came over and said so. He was awful. He said terrible things. He'll hurt them. I know he will."

"Les? Are you talking about Les?" Patiently, Todd questioned me until I had told him the entire story. Then he said, "I'll go over there right now and settle this."

"No. Don't go. He's drunk. He's a crazy man. I just want to get away from here. I don't want to stay anywhere near him. Let's sell the house and go somewhere else. Please. Please, let's just go."

Todd soothed and quieted me. "This isn't the time to make a major decision," he said. "Let's wait until we're both calmer. Then we'll talk about it."

Together we went to the girls' room. We looked at them. Todd bent to kiss them in their sleep. I straightened their covers and lingered, not wanting to leave them. Finally, we went to our own room.

We did decide to sell our house. The darkness in the house across the street frightened and oppressed us. We ran away from our neighbors in order to preserve ourselves and our children. It was, we thought, the rational course of action.

CHAPTER

THIRTY · THREE

———————— 🍇 ————————

One day, when she was nearly seventy, my mother told us that she was leaving the apartment where she had lived alone, happily, for many years. She was moving into a church retirement home in a nearby town. She had put her name on the waiting list eight years before without telling us.

My husband and I were aghast. "But Mother," I protested, "we've told you. We want you to come to us when you don't want to be alone anymore."

She was adamant. "I've made up my mind. It will work out beautifully. I want you to see the place. Then you'll know what I mean."

Todd and I took the girls and went with Mother one day to inspect The Home, as we came to call it. Meg and Alice, with their dolls and doll clothes, sat in a sunny patio and played while Todd and I toured the establishment with Mother and the director.

It was beautiful. Set in park-like grounds, far back from the street, under old sycamores and oaks, the buildings looked as if they truly belonged there.

We saw the room Mother would have. We inspected the communal living and dining rooms, furnished comfortably with a mixture of the antique and the contemporary. We visited the library, the auditorium, the chapel.

When we went out to get the girls, Meg said, "A lot of grannies talked to us. It's a nice place."

Alice asked, "Is Granny going to live here?"

"Yes."

"Can we come and see her?"

"Yes. Often."

"Will she still come and see us?"

"Of course."

We helped her move in. She took a few of her own things: her rocking chair, the print of Raphael's "Madonna of the Chair" that had always hung above our tilt-back table. She took her Bible and some of her books and a silver vase my father had given her as an anniversary gift many years ago.

So she settled in. She made new friends. She took part in excursions planned for the Home family, and soon knew herself to be part of a close-knit community.

Every week Todd drove over to get her so that she could have Sunday dinner and the afternoon with us. She went to the early service in her Home chapel. We went to service at our own church. She always seemed to enjoy our family meal, visiting with us, playing with the girls and various and sundry assorted kittens. Late in the afternoon we'd drive her home again, the girls snuggled beside her in the back seat.

One day, in her room, she had a little stroke. "I felt myself falling," she told us later, "and I touched my intercom switch as I fell." A nurse was with her in minutes and she was in the infirmary almost before she realized what had happened.

We relaxed then. It was better than we could have done for her when she was alone in her apartment. And we gave thanks that she was in a secure and gracious place.

She lived there more than twenty years. "I never regretted my decision for one minute," she told us.

My mother changed during those years. She had always been a serious, dignified woman. But in her last years she developed a mischievous kind of sparkle that I had not seen before.

Often that sparkle, that controlled hilarity, was directed toward herself. But sometimes her target was God. It seems to me that God must be the recipient of little enough hilarity. I believe that my mother's, offered with great good will, must have been acceptable.

There is an old German carol called "Hilariter." One of the stanzas says:

And all you living things make praise,
   Hilariter, hilariter;
He guideth you on all your ways,
   Alleluya, alleluya.

The carol rings in my mind as I think of a day when I took her to have her eyes checked. Her vision was growing more blurred. We waited a long time in the crowded office. After a while Mother said, loudly, as deaf people often speak, "Dear, are we in a hurry?"

"No, Mother."

"Would we have time to drop by the chapel when you take me home, so I can say my prayers?"

Papers and magazines began to rustle as waiting patients peeked around them at my mother. Only slightly embarrassed I said, "Of course we can."

With that unique twinkle in her bright blue eyes, their inner vision unclouded by the exterior film, she said, a good deal more loudly than she needed to, "Good. I wonder what God would like to hear today. There's not much for us to talk about anymore, you know. We know each other so well. I could say the Lord's Prayer, of course, but He must hear that so often."

We did stop at the chapel before I took her to her room, and we were quiet there together for a few moments. And then, when she was settled on her own bed to rest awhile before her suppertime she said, "I want to talk to you about something."

"Yes, Mother?"

"Look in my top dresser drawer. There's a note for you."

I found the note.

"Don't read it now. I'll tell you about it and you can read it later. It's about my funeral. I picked out the hymns I'd like to have, and the psalms and prayers. And I'd like to be buried beside Karl."

"Mother," I began, not knowing exactly what I was going to say. My inner voice was saying *Not yet. Please, not yet.*

She stopped me. "It's nothing to be sad about. You are to have the Raphael and my mother's cameo. It's all there, in the note. And there are a few things for Meg and Alice." She smiled, her eyes sparkling again as they had in the doctor's office.

"What, Mother? What are you thinking about?"

"Dying is nothing to be alarmed about. Not at my age. If people can get to the moon, why should I have problems getting to heaven? I have perfect faith in the arrangements."

Between laughter and tears, I kissed her. "I'll see you later," I told her.

She patted my hand. "Yes." She smiled. "One way or another."

CHAPTER
THIRTY · FOUR

———— 🍇 ————

I poured my husband's coffee, looking over his shoulder at the headlines. "It's all so grim," I said. Then I called, "Girls. Breakfast is ready."

"It's grim, all right," Todd agreed, as he continued reading.

"Mommie," Meg ran into the room, sat down at her place, and gulped her orange juice. "You won't forget the cookies for the Talent Show tonight, will you? The whole sixth grade's counting on you."

I suppose that's something, I thought. *The world is in a state of chaos, and the sixth grade is counting on me to make cookies.* To Meg I said, "Okay. Chocolate chip."

Eight-year-old Alice came in and sat at her place at the table. "Daddy, I need a current event and you have the paper. Can you find one for me?"

I looked across at Todd. "What will you give her? War, riots, poverty, pollution?"

"I'd rather have one about ecology," Alice said.

"Mommie," Meg asked, "do you think you'll have my new dress finished by tonight?" Without waiting for an answer she turned to her father. "Daddy, tonight's the Talent Show. Don't forget. It's really important."

"I'll be there." Todd smiled across Meg at me. "'Bye, flock." He kissed everyone and started for the door, handing Alice a piece of the paper as he went. "Here's one about ecology," he said. "Be sure to read it yourself before you use it. See you all later."

"Thanks, Daddy." Alice was eating her egg.

"Come on, pokey, we'll miss the bus," Meg said.

"Don't call me pokey." Alice finished her egg and carefully wiped her mouth.

Meg moistened the corner of a napkin and scrubbed at a spot Alice had missed. "There. You're fine. Come on, slowpoke."

"Don't call me slowpoke." Alice picked up her lunch box and followed Meg out the door.

I waved to them from the window and turned back to the kitchen mess. Deciding to ignore it for a moment, I warmed the coffee and looked at the paper while I had another cup. *Sometimes I think I'd rather not read it at all,* I thought. *But that's no good, either. All those awful things are there. You can't just hide from them. And they're all so large. Nothing's small anymore. Except maybe my own world.*

The phone rang. "Julie?" It was Wendy, next door. She sounded excited. "Are you going to be home awhile? Lou still isn't well enough to go back to school, and I've been called for a job interview."

"I'll be home. I have to make cookies for school tonight."

"Thanks. She'll be okay for a while alone. I'll tell her not to call unless she has a real emergency."

"Fine. I'll be right here." I had put the first batch of cookies in the oven when the doorbell rang. There stood five-year-old Lou in her bathrobe, her brown eyes enormous, her lip quivering.

"Hi, Lou. You're not supposed to be out, are you?"

"Mrs. Ashton." Lou's voice was shaky. "Mrs. Ashton, is it an emergency when you're so lonesome you're going to cry?"

I leaned to hug her. "Honey, that's the worst kind of emergency." I settled Lou in a sunny spot in the kitchen and we chatted while I worked. When I heard Wendy drive in next door I went out and called to her. "Lou's here. She got lonesome."

Wendy came in. "Baby, you weren't supposed to go out." She took a deep breath. "Those cookies smell heavenly."

I put out cookies and milk. "How did it go?"

"Great," she said. "It's just the kind of job I want. Dan isn't too excited about my going back to work, but I'm so restless I can't wait to get back into it."

"Into what, Mommie?" Lou's mouth was rimmed with milk.

"The great big world, baby." Then she turned to me. "What do you think? Really, I mean."

"I think you have to make up your own mind."

"Well, it's time for this one's medicine," Wendy said. "Thanks, Julie. We'll see you later."

All the rest of the day, as I finished the hem of Meg's new dress, as I packed the cookies, pressed Alice's jumper, and listened to the news on the radio, I thought of the contrast between my own activities and the vast concerns of the world. *It's not that I don't care about doing something real,* I thought. *It's just that I never have the time to do more than I do. And the PTA and the League of Women Voters just don't seem to be exclusively crucial right now.*

The rest of the day progressed busily but smoothly. Somehow everything got done, and it was time to dress.

"May I use some of your bath oil? Just tonight?"

"Just tonight, Meg. Only a few drops."

"Mother." Alice materialized in my bedroom. "I need my pink blouse with the long sleeves."

I stared at her. "Honey, I didn't get it ironed."

Alice looked solemn. "I really need it with my jumper. You told me not to try to iron that one. Remember? But I really need it." Alice never coaxed or whined. She simply stated facts, as she saw them.

179

I was pressing the blouse when Meg came to me. "I'm through with the bathroom." Her hair was curly from the steam of the bath, and her cheeks were glowing.

She's going to be beautiful, I thought. *She's going to be a beautiful woman.* I was filled with a rush of love for this family of mine. *How can I help them? How can Todd and I build a bridge from this safe home out into that terrifying world? They have to live in it.*

"Don't look so worried, Mommie," Meg said. "I'm not going to make any mistakes."

I didn't understand.

"Tonight, I mean. And even if I do make a mistake, I can probably fix it. Don't worry."

I hugged her. "You'll be great."

At the school we took the cookies to Meg's room and she went backstage in the auditorium while the three of us found our seats. Alice settled back with a contented little wiggle. "I just love this blouse."

I grinned at her. "I know you do."

Promptly at seven-thirty the principal stepped to the stage and said, "We are pleased to present our annual sixth-grade Talent Show. I should like to introduce the student who made most of the arrangements for the evening and who will serve as our announcer: Meg Ashton."

I gasped. Alice said, "I didn't tell, did I? I promised Meg. I didn't tell."

"Nobody told me a thing." I took Alice's hand in one of mine and Todd's in the other.

Meg stood there poised and confident. She said, "This program is dedicated to our parents because they're the people we just can't get along without." It seemed to me that Meg smiled right at us, and then she announced the first number.

Children sang, danced, played their guitars, and then all of them grouped together for the finale. As they began to sing, I suddenly saw them through a glimmer of tears. *Do they still sing it,* I thought, *in spite of everything?*

> *Long may our land be bright*
> *With freedom's holy light . . .*

I reminded myself that the world evolved slowly, a day at a time, everything in its place. *And that's the way we have to do our work. Every day we build part of that bridge, Todd and I. We help them build a bridge from their small world to the big one. Carefully. Lovingly. A day at a time.*

CHAPTER

THIRTY • FIVE

❦

When the girls were grown, I returned to teaching. We were a diverse group in that college classroom: the students, ranging in age from eighteen to sixty, and ranging in their spiritual stances from professed atheist (Jim, nineteen) to evangelistic Christian (Emma, fifty-plus) and I . . . wife, grandmother, teacher, listener, searcher. And it was in that classroom, toward the end of a semester, that I had a sudden insight into the possibilities of a contemporary Pentecost.

From the beginning Emma irritated Jim and Jim made Emma desperate. Our class, a workshop for writers, was supposed to maintain a collectively open mind. We would, we decided, never criticize subject matter, never censor content. We could concern ourselves with technique and with the development of style.

But Emma's poems were usually prayers. They addressed God directly and they were often either preachy or sentimental, or both. Jim would scream about these qualities and we would have to agree with him that a subtler approach reaches out to readers more successfully. Besides, Jim would say, he *didn't believe any of that stuff.*

I would warn, *Watch it. You're criticizing personal attitude and content.*

Emma would agonize over Jim's stories. They were usually competent. They were always totally realistic. They involved gangs, drug users, prostitutes. They were graphic and sometimes filled with obscene language.

Why do you want to write about that kind of thing? Emma would wail.

And I would say, *Watch it. You're criticizing content and personal attitude.*

In a group such as ours, when the preoccupation is with the development of artistic expression, there is a gradual welding, somehow, and the group becomes interactive. When any one person is absent there is a weakening of fabric, and we all lose.

Jim returned to us after a two weeks' absence. Emma said, wholeheartedly, *I missed you.* She sounded surprised at her own words.

Jim looked first amazed and then pleased. He had been to his father's funeral, he told us, in New Jersey. His father had walked out on the family when Jim was small, but he and Jim had always kept in touch. So Jim had borrowed the money to go to the funeral. And, he wanted to know, did Emma *really believe all that stuff about . . . you know . . . heaven, and everything?*

Emma said *Yes!*

Jim, with a sheepish grin, admitted that she had a right to her beliefs. Who could tell? There might be something in them.

Praise God, said Emma.

Watch it, said Jim.

Relaxed laughter from everyone, a pervading warmth, as of benevolent tongues of flame, and Pentecost happened. It happened there in a classroom in January, when we understood each other, each in his own language, even in our diversity.

CHAPTER
THIRTY · SIX

———————— ❦ ————————

Tragedy, high and irreversible as that of any Greek drama, took place one spring night, and I didn't even know. Oh, I heard about it on the late news on television. The newscaster announced, between items of world importance, that a man had been shot and killed in the Silverlake district of Los Angeles.

I heard him say it. I heard him, and I didn't think about it again. I didn't know anyone in the Silverlake area. This murder of a nameless man had nothing to do with me, my family, or our friends.

After the newscast we put the dog in, locked the house, turned off the lights and went to bed. We slept all night in peace and safety.

But early the next morning our telephone rang.

In Greek drama the tragic action occurs off-stage and the news is brought by a messenger. Our messenger was the secretary at St. Paul's, our parish church.

"I have sad news," she said. "Evan Nielson was shot and killed last night in the Silverlake district in Los Angeles."

Evan. Evan Neilson, the organist-choirmaster at our church, is a musician of power and stature.

Was.

Was. I can still hardly say it. He had just completed his doctoral dissertation for Julliard School of Music. His career lay ahead of him, promising and bright. He was thirty-two.

And then, *in an instant, in the twinkling of an eye* the promise was broken, the music silenced. Bach and Handel, Widor and Dupré will have to speak through other hands, other intellects. And silence is our portion.

A few days later we took part in the service that celebrated Evan's life and commemorated his death. Someone else played the organ. The choir he had trained sang for him one last time. His young body was committed to the earth, his soul to heaven. We listened to the comforting, strengthening words. In our grief we supported each other.

But there remains a question I continue to ask myself, a question for which I have not yet found an answer, though much time has passed.

How could I not have grieved when that matter-of-fact voice told us the news late that night?

Has violence become so ordinary, so common among us, that I do not even react when I hear of senseless death? React with pain, no matter who has died?

Violent acts are prevalent as weeds. We hear about them and the words drift like mist out of our consciousness. We skirt the dark corners of our own lives, trying to elude the ominous voices of danger. We grow numb. We protect ourselves by saying *These things happen*. But they happen to others, not to us. Not to me. Not to you. Not to those we love.

They are supposed to happen to the unknown Other.

But Evan was that Other.

I heard that he had died. The messenger announced the anonymous death. I heard it.

It was my friend, Evan, who died.

I heard the news.

And I didn't even listen.

CHAPTER
THIRTY • SEVEN

There she was, one of the youngest new ones in my children's choir. About nine, Polly was then, and about as big as three minutes. She was fair with two long pigtails and bright blue eyes that held mischief and intelligence.

I greeted the children on this first rehearsal of the new season, explained rehearsal procedures, attendance requirements. Polly grinned at me, not impudently, but as if she knew a secret that was tickling her almost past endurance.

At the end of that first session Polly's older choir sister, the one I had assigned to guide and help her in her first year, said, "Polly has a really good voice. And she didn't have any trouble reading the words and the notes. She'll be fine. But . . ."

"What?"

"I don't know. I think she's about ready to explode. Maybe she's just happy."

Polly never missed a rehearsal or a Sunday service. One day after our Thursday afternoon practice she said, "Mrs. Ashton, could you give me a ride home today? My mom has to work late, and she can't pick me up."

So began our Thursday afternoon rides together. I dropped her off on my way home. The conversation was always stimulating. It was good to be reminded of nine-year-old interests. And later, of ten, eleven, twelve, and thirteen-year-old concerns.

On a certain Thursday, eleven-year-old Polly said, "I'm in the school orchestra. Bet you can't guess what instrument."

"Flute? Piccolo?" They seemed about the right size, somehow.

That unique chuckle. "Nope. Guess again."

"Violin?"

"Nope. Trombone." Now the laugh was hearty, full of secret pleasure.

The thought of the small girl managing the clumsy instrument intrigued me. "Why trombone?" I asked, parking in front of her house.

That chortle again. "Because I can sit behind a boy and poke him and everybody thinks it's an accident."

Next came swimming. She became a champion swimmer in grade school, middle school, high school. And all the while she sang in the choir, her braids growing longer, her eyes losing none of their gleam.

"I've decided what I want to be," she told me one day shortly before her graduation from high school. "Guess."

"An athlete? A coach?"

"Nope. Try again."

"A musician?" She had long since given up the trombone, and by now she was a proficient pianist.

"No. Don't laugh. I want to be a vet. I love animals. I think I'd be good at taking care of them. Animals you can trust. Mostly."

When she went away to college I could not believe that the years had passed so quickly. She became involved in science. Her notes to me were full of the joy of her experiences.

She came to church one Christmas Eve. Now her hair was in one long braid. She wore a blue dress. She smiled at me, but I felt something missing in her eyes. They didn't meet mine with their usual clarity, although I felt that she was glad to see me. We embraced. She felt so thin.

"Are you all right?" I asked her, after we had exchanged Christmas greetings.

"Sure."

"Good." But I was uneasy. I wrote to her, asking how things really were.

She answered, *I guess I'm okay. I've given up the idea of being a vet. I'm into work as a medical lab technician. I guess that's what I want to do. All of it's hard. I don't get home much anymore. Homework, you know.*

The years avalanched. Polly graduated from the university. She got a fine position in a medical laboratory in Los Angeles. I didn't see her again, but I always heard from her at Christmas, and I always wrote to her. Her parents reported her progress, her success.

Then one day I came home after spending a weekend in retreat at Mt. Calvary, the monastery high on a hill above Santa Barbara. I was filled with a sense of well-being, of renewal, of peace.

"I have bad news for you," Todd said, after he had greeted me.

I braced myself. Our daughters? Our granddaughter?

He said abruptly, "Polly is dead."

I looked at him in unbelief.

"It's true," he said. "She was found at the bottom of an elevator shaft in a Los Angeles building. They don't know what happened. The police are working on it."

"Oh, not Polly! Not that kind of death." The smiling, mischievous child, so in love with life. The good student, the successful career woman.

We went to see Polly's parents, but they were not at home. So I wrote to them, vainly trying to express my grief, knowing how deep theirs must be.

I served at Polly's funeral. The church was full. By the grace of God I was able to read the great words of St. Paul without stumbling. I was able to pray aloud for Polly's family, for all of us who would miss her.

When I talked to Polly's mother, some time after, she told me quietly, "Polly was very different inside from the picture she presented to the world. She couldn't handle her life, somehow. She couldn't cope. She must have been confused and uncontrolled when she fell down that shaft. Somehow she just couldn't cope with her life."

All those years I had seen Polly and thought of her as the merry, carefree child I had first known. How did I miss it? That Christmas Eve when she said she was all right, should I have known that she wasn't all right at all? Should I have read between the lines of her letters?

My rector told me that I couldn't have known. There was nothing I could have done. There was nothing he could do. He tried. Her parents tried. Something mysterious went wrong. A hidden something.

Still, I grieve for her, and I try to forgive myself. There remains a Polly-shaped absence in my life. And I hope that, in the words of the Book of Common Prayer, she has received pardon and rest, that she is going from strength to strength. That she is becoming Polly, as she was always meant to be.

CHAPTER

THIRTY · EIGHT

It's pleasant to linger over another cup of coffee after Todd has left for work in the morning. I look at the California oaks and the sycamores that bend over the house across the street, and I think how lucky we are to have this kind of view from the dining room window. I've hung a hummingbird feeder on a branch of the large oak that shades our house.

I'm amused at the persistence of a certain bird. Nearly every morning he sits for a while on a small branch near the feeder and sounds his metallic imperative, the scarlet iridescence of his throat blazing like a little flame. The other birds don't try to use the feeder while he is there protecting his territory.

The telephone rings. Eight o'clock on a Monday morning is early for a call, even in this house where the telephone rings often.

"It's your mother, Mrs. Ashton," the voice says. "I'm afraid it's bad this time. She's very ill. Can you come?" It is a nurse calling from the infirmary of the retirement home where my mother lives.

I can't reach Todd, so I leave him a note. I seem to do everything in slow motion. As I dress and write the note, as I lock doors and start the car, my mind is grappling with the possibility of finality for my mother. She is in her ninetieth year. People say, *How fortunate you are to have had her with you so long.* To be sure. But surely it is not yet time for us to lose her?

I have observed the metamorphosis of my mother, her emergence from shadow to sunlight. Her true delight has been in grandmothering, and her closeness to Meg and Alice has been a joy to watch. Now she is godmother to her great-grandchild, Meg's Jennifer. I am greedy on my mother's behalf. I want her to have the joy of watching this child grow. Now is this possibility to be threatened?

In times of crisis one who is directly involved in the crisis feels isolated, forsaken. Ordinary occurrences run parallel to one's involvement with crisis. People read papers, drive cars, go to school, to work. Traffic lights change from red to green to amber to red. No one notices that you are caught in the grip of terrible pain.

As I drive to the infirmary, it seems heartless that the drivers of cars passing me or pulling up beside me at lights do not share my concern. The pedestrians I wait for, school children laughing and chasing each other, businessmen, how insensitive they are to the anguish I feel. Even the highway patrol car that passes me. I want to stop the driver and say, *Do something. It's my mother.* But I am alone.

When I arrive I park in the parking lot, lock the car, and walk in the back door. It is all mechanical. And then, in my mother's room, I stand looking down at her. Her eyes are closed and she is lying very still. They have combed her hair into one long braid. When she is well her hair is silver, shining, crackling with life. Now it is heavy and dull. Her hands lie quiet. Usually they are active, an eloquent part of her conversations. Today they have no life of their own. Thin, bony, splotched with brown, they could belong to any old woman. Even the gold wedding band has no special meaning today. It is like any other.

If only I could see her eyes. Intensely blue, they sparkle with pleasure, with interest, with the laughter she so often aims at herself, especially when she forgets things she thinks she should remember.

One day recently she startled me. I had come to see her, bringing a bunch of violets from our yard. She took the flowers, delightedly smelling them, touching them. Then she looked at me and asked my name. I must have looked stricken because, almost at once she said, "Julie. Of course, it's you. For just a moment there . . . it must have been the light."

Before I left her that day, she laughed about it. "I don't know what's happened to my mind," she said. "Sometimes it behaves as if it belongs to someone else. Some old lady I don't know, don't even want to know."

Just remembering that, I smile. As I stand there, smiling, the nurse moves forward to check on my mother.

"Am I in your way?" I ask her.

"No, thanks, Mrs. Ashton. You're fine."

I sit beside my mother as the morning inches along. This room is pleasant, its colors soft and warm. Through a window I see sycamores and eucalyptus trees moving in the air. It has begun to cloud over now. Perhaps there will be rain. Time is going on everywhere, just as it always does, no matter what happens to anyone.

My mother stirs. Her fingers move against the sheet. I take her cold hand in my own warm one. She opens her eyes slowly, as if the lids are heavy. She struggles to focus on my face. "Julie?"

"Yes, Mother. I'm right here."

She sighs. "What has happened?" She looks at me and then closes her eyes again.

"You're in the infirmary."

"I smell roses."

"Yes. The gardener sent them to you. Would you like to hold one so you can smell it better?"

She nods. I break the thorns off a red rose and put it into her hand. She tries to lift it, to smell it, but she is too weak. I lay it on her pillow.

Then, abruptly, she asks, "Where's Jen?"

Jen is her mother. My grandmother. She died forty years ago. I hesitate.

She repeats, "Where's Jen?"

"You remember, Mother," I say quietly. "Jen has been gone a long time. You remember."

She sleeps again after a while. I step out to the coffee shop for some lunch. She is still sleeping when I return. All through the afternoon she sleeps, her thin chest barely rising and falling with her rapid breathing. I have read somewhere that when memory goes, it is the most recent memory that fades first. Then there is a sort of peeling process, and one is finally left with an acute memory of the distant past. My mother has had to ask me my name, but she thinks of her own mother as living.

"Mrs. Ashton?" It is one of the nurses.

"Yes."

"There's a phone call for you. You may take it at the desk."

It's Todd. "I just got home and read your note. I'm so sorry you couldn't reach me. How is she?" His voice is deep and kind. I feel better, just hearing it.

"She's very weak. Dr. Houghton isn't sure yet just how serious it is. She's no longer in any pain, but she's so weak."

"I'm going to have some supper and keep an appointment. Then I'll ask someone to drive me over there later so that I can bring you home. You'll be tired. It's been a long day for you."

"That will be wonderful, darling. Thanks. I don't want to leave her yet. She may wake again, and I want to be here. Oh, Todd, she's so frail."

"She's seemed frail for a long time, but she's surprised us before. Give her my love when she wakes up, will you? And I'll see you later."

He's right. She does have surprising reserves of strength. And she has needed them. She used to say, *We've got to have some steel in our backbones.* And she has.

One of the nurses brings me a supper tray. "We thought you might like to eat in here, Mrs. Ashton. It looks good, doesn't it?"

"Very good," I agree, suddenly hungry. In addition to the tray there's a paper plate holding a piece of cake that is decorated with pink sugar roses. "That looks like birthday cake," I say.

"It is. Little Mrs. Pendleton in the next room is ninety today. Her family brought a cake. She and your mother are friends, you know, and she wanted to share her cake." She takes my mother's pulse. Going out quietly she says, "Enjoy your supper."

Soon my mother wakes again. "Julie?"

"Yes, Mother. I'm here."

"I'm so thirsty."

I help her sip some cool water through a plastic tube. She lies back with a sigh. Glancing in the direction of my tray she says, "That looks like birthday cake."

"It is. Today is Mrs. Pendleton's birthday. She sent us a piece of her cake."

"Ninety today, Mrs. Pendleton," my mother says. "I was planning to come over here and see her. Well, I came, didn't I? But not for her birthday."

She seems alert now, aware of everything. This must be a good sign. "Todd called, Mother. He sent you his love."

"That's nice. Give him mine, too."

"You can do that yourself. He's coming over later."

"I wish I could see Martin," she says. "It's been so long."

I take her hand. For a long time she says nothing more. The room is growing dark, but I do not turn on a light. I sit watching her. Flat and slight under the covers, she seems to be fading even as I look at her. *Mother, Mother,* I beg her silently, *It isn't time. Not yet.*

Outside the trees move in a rising wind. Then with a rustling sound against the screen, rain begins to fall. Soon it is falling with force. I hope she will hear it. She has always loved the sound of rain.

The nurse comes in again. My mother responds when we speak to her. "Mother," I say. "Listen. Do you hear the rain?"

"I'm not dreaming?" she asks.

I open the window so that the sound is clear, the freshness of the air closer to all of us.

"I'm glad," my mother says.

The nurse gives her an injection. "This is to give you a good night, Mrs. Erlich," she tells my mother. "Sweet dreams now."

I take my mother's hand. She whispers something I do not hear. "What did you say?" I ask, bending down to her.

She smiles at me and whispers, "I'll see you later."

I sit in the dark as she sleeps, thinking, remembering. I am startled to feel hands on my shoulders. Todd has come into the room. I take his hand. "I'm glad you're here."

Todd looks at my mother. "How is she? Is there any change?"

I stand and, turning away from my mother I say to Todd, "She isn't going to get better this time. I know it."

"Let's go home," Todd says, holding out my coat. He has brought my boots and umbrella. "It's time to go home."

I look at my mother, sleeping on the white, impersonal bed. I lean to kiss her. She doesn't move. "Good night," I whisper. "Good night."

As we pass the nursing station the nurse says, "I'll be watching her. Don't worry, now, Mrs. Ashton. You get some rest. You look as if you need it."

"Call me if you need me," I say, and she promises.

At home I have a hot bath and a cup of tea that Todd has brewed. He's made toast, too, and it tastes good. I relax, comfortable in my night clothes, in my own home. We stand at the window for a long moment, looking out at the rain. The oaks bend under its weight. Water slants across the windows, driven by the force of the wind. At last we go to bed.

Lying in the circle of Todd's arms I begin to cry. He holds me, whispering things I can scarcely hear. But the pressure of his arms, the tangible quality of his comfort soothe me, and soon I stop crying.

"You have to be ready to let her go," Todd says. "You know that. You must be willing to let her go. You don't want her to have more times like this one. I know you don't. You just have to let her go."

He's right. But how can I simply decide to let her go? In spite of my grief and fatigue I realize that a melody has been going through my mind all day, all evening. And now, trying to compose my thoughts, I know what it is. "Oh God, Our Help in Ages Past." But the words that have been persisting in the back of my consciousness are from a later verse:

Time, like an ever-rolling stream
Bears all its sons away.

Its daughters, too, I think, as sleep washes over me. When at last I fall into sleep, it is as if I slip into the clear, cool waters of the lake. My dreams are of the island. Of Father and Martin singing and laughing together. Of Mother in her blue dress, light falling on her smooth brown hair. She smiles, touches me, and says, *I'll see you later.*

Later, I do not know how much later, I struggle up from the waters, hearing an insistent sound. Heavy with sleep, I recognize the sound as the ringing of the telephone. The dial on the clock says four. The telephone rings on and on.

Then Todd answers it. "Yes," he says. "Yes. I see. Thank you. Yes, of course. I'll tell her. Good-bye."

He looks at me and I know this is not a dream. I am awake and I know what he is going to tell me.

CHAPTER
THIRTY · NINE

O ne hot California day, the first week in November, I drove to the city near our home. Christmas had arrived. The shops were full of imposing artificial trees decorated with plastic ornaments. Beautifully wrapped packages were displayed on elegantly draped tables. I suspected that the boxes were empty. Musak insisted upon joy to this materialistic world.

I rapidly became what our younger daughter, Alice, calls "all out of gruntle." Parking spaces were scarce, the stores were crowded with people whose faces were tense and strained. Clerks were snappish. Santa, in his shoddy red costume and false white beard, was on every corner. I could not find the things I thought I had to buy. My feet hurt.

Finally, walking toward still another store, I passed a large church. Noticing a sign that was taped to the great front door, I went up to read it. Printed in neat letters, the sign read, *This Church Will Not Be Open Christmas Day.*

Those words kept repeating themselves in my mind as I walked to my car, as I drove home, frustrated and disgruntled. That evening I wrote this poem:

Villanelle for Christmas

I read the sign upon a carved oak door:
This Church Will Not Be Open Christmas Day.
Our Father doesn't live here anymore?

The traffic sounds like any jungle roar;
The animals have all come out to play.
I read the sign upon a carved oak door.

Come, Christian soldiers, marching as to war,
Heigh-ho the holly. Deck the halls. Be gay.
Our Father doesn't live here anymore.

If man wants something special to adore,
the price is right. Sometimes there's hell to pay.
I read the sign upon a carved oak door.

Shepherds and wise men, what was the journey for?
Your Love rose up, and then he went away.
Our Father doesn't live here anymore.

Hark, Herald Angels, hovering to explore
our silent sleep, this peaceful Christmas Day,
I read a sign upon a carved oak door.
Our Father doesn't live here anymore.

I realize that my poem is angry, cynical, bitter. I am almost sorry that I had written it, that it was printed. The poem arose out of the frustration and disillusionment I had been suffering that morning. I felt myself to be caught in the secular trap.

And yet, it is a season the world keeps, and I am part of the secular world. So the trick must be to achieve a balance between both worlds, the secular and that other that we are sometimes loath to name.

So, during the next weeks, those Advent weeks before Christmas, we tried to gain and keep that balance. The preparations . . . baking, cleaning, shopping, wrapping, mailing, decorating . . . were accomplished with the thought that somehow they would lead us to the season of love that we call Christmas.

The cards went out with a handwritten note on each, however brief. We wanted to reinforce the fragile connection that links us to distant friends. We tried to do all that we did not because we thought we had to, but because we wanted to, for love's sake.

❄ ❄ ❄

And now it is the day before Christmas Eve. Our older daughter, Meg, and her husband, Jerry, with Jennifer, our small granddaughter, are driving down from the Pacific Northwest to be with us. They will have driven more than a thousand miles, and they will be tired when they arrive.

Our house looks, smells, sounds festive. The Christmas tree touches the ceiling. It would probably not please an interior decorator, but it pleases us. Some of the ornaments are new this year. We collect musical instruments . . . miniature trumpets, lutes, violins. Some of the ornaments have belonged to the tree from the time our girls were born, left at this house to hang on our tree year after year. Some, like me, are a bit the worse for wear. They were on my first tree. We have decorated this tree, as we always do, to the music of Bach, Handel, Pachelbel, and to the sound of medieval carols. It is more than a tree. It is an icon, for it recalls the tree of life.

All day a huge pot of soup has been simmering, and it will be ready whenever our travelers arrive. The cookies are baked, the breads ready. The house contains the elements of ceremony, and we are waiting. This waiting is for our mortal family, and by means of it we feel that we are part of that greater expectation.

Dusk comes early. We turn on the Christmas tree lights and the lights that illuminate the small pine tree on our back hill. We turn on porch lights. Then the three of us,

Todd and I and Alice, wait by the light of tapers, tree, and fire.

At last Sammie, our venerable collie, barks. It is her joyful, welcoming bark. We hear a rush of tires on the driveway. We hurry out into the crisp air, Jennifer explodes from the car and runs toward us, and we are engulfed in love.

Soon, after the initial jubilance of greetings, we gather round the table, hold hands, and say our thanks. Candles flicker, the soup steams. Fresh bread and cheese nourish us. It is an *agape* feast.

Jennifer falls asleep with a winter pear in her hand. She does not waken when her mother undresses her and carries her to bed. Exhausted from their journey, Jennifer's parents go to bed, too. Alice goes to the hospital, for she is working the night shift. Todd and I companionably do the dishes and then we sit together while the fire burns down.

When we go to bed it is still Advent. Outside in the dark the stars are singing.

❋ ❋ ❋

On the morning of Christmas Eve the house is full of secrets. There are bustlings, laughter, whispered conversations. Packages appear, mysteriously, under the tree. In patched blue jeans, a Sesame Street tee shirt and, inexplicably, one pink and one orange slipper, Jennifer stands, head back, staring at the top of the Christmas tree.

"Nana?"

"Yes, Jennifer?"

"That Baby Jesus up there at the top. Is he really the same Jesus who was on your tree when you were a little girl?"

"Yes."

"The same one that was on my mother's tree when she was a little girl? And Aunt Alice's?"

"Yes. The same."

She studies the small cardboard Child in a crib. It is always at the top of our tree. It came from Germany from my father's parents before my first Christmas. Every year we wrap it carefully in tissue paper before we put it away. It is liberally patched with tape. But the sweet face of the Child, his raised hand, have not changed.

"Will he be there forever?" Jennifer asks.

"Yes," I say.

Somehow, with jobs and stories and lunch and bath, the hours of the day avalanche. Toward twilight, Jennifer and her parents go to the family service at St. Paul's while Todd and I get dinner.

Jennifer returns full of news.

She carried a banner in the procession.

There was a real, live baby in the crèche and he smiled when the children stood there watching him.

She sang "Away in a Manger" with all the others.

Afterwards, in a big room, there was a piñata for all the children.

She shows us her red balloon and a small bag of candies.

We take her picture standing in front of the tree. She wears a red velvet jumper and a white blouse with frills at the throat and wrists. She is so like the child her mother was that I am almost confused.

Tonight as we hold hands around the table we sing, at Jennifer's request, part of "Angels We Have Heard on High" as our Grace. Todd carves the turkey. Jennifer eats a few bites of white meat. She eats several olives and all the cherries from her fruit salad. She breaks into song spontaneously. "Deck the halls with boughs of folly."

Soon she asks to be excused. The rest of us linger at the table, talking until the candles burn down. Jennifer soon reappears dressed in pajamas, robe, and a pair of socks. She carries her slippers, one pink, one orange.

"What happened to your slippers?" Alice asks her. "Why don't they match?"

Jennifer giggles. "Well . . . me and Robin . . ."

"Robin and I," Meg interrupts.

"Yes. Robin and I, we stayed over at Robin's house and we got our slippers mixed up. But me and Robin's stuff fits each other, so we don't care."

Meg groans. But it is not a night on which to be overly concerned about syntax.

Jennifer asks me for a plate of cookies and a glass of milk. She and her father put them on the hearth with the slippers beside them. If all goes well, Santa will have a midnight snack, take her (and Robin's) slippers and leave new ones.

Meanwhile she is excited. She goes from one to another of us. "Mother, do I have to go to bed?"

"Yes. But not quite yet."

"Daddy, are you excited?"

"Yes," he says. "Why, aren't you?"

She jumps. "I am. I can't wait." She goes to Alice. "Auntie Alice, why don't you have a little girl?"

"You know why. I'm not married. But I have you, part of the time." They embrace. "I miss you when you aren't here."

"I know. Do you like to be a nurse?"

"Yes. Most of the time."

Jennifer goes to lean on the arm of her grandfather's chair. "Papa, are you excited?"

Todd yawns. "Yes. Are you?"

Jumping again she says, "I can't wait." She thinks a moment. "Tomorrow I get to open the last door. You know. In my Advent calendar that you and Nana sent me. I know what's in there. The Baby Jesus. Because tomorrow's his birthday. Right?"

"Right."

She comes to me. "Nana, why don't you have any mother?"

"My mother is in heaven. She was your great grandmother."

"I know. My mother's Nana. But she called her Granny."

It is still difficult for me to realize that I am the matriarch of this family. What has happened to time? My own childhood is clear and immediate in my mind. And here is my grandchild, climbing up onto my lap.

"Tell me about the time when I was scared of the dark. When I was three." She settles back, her hand in mine. Her hand is like her mother's and like my own, the fingers long and slender, the palm wide. I hold this small bundle of energy, frail flesh, delicate white bone, boundless spirit. Jennifer, daughter of our daughter.

I begin, "One night when you were very small . . ."

She stops me. "Start, 'Once upon a time.' "

I obey. "Once upon a time when you were three, you woke up in the night and you were afraid. The shadows in your room looked like THINGS, and you were afraid of them. So your parents took you outdoors."

"My daddy carried me."

"Yes."

"Just like Papa carried my mother when she was your little girl."

"Just like that," I agree. "Your daddy carried you outside, and it was moonlight. 'Look,' he said to you, 'that's a branch of the apple tree. It makes a pattern on your bedroom wall.' And your mother said, 'Look. See the clothes line? It makes a shadow on your curtain.'

"They walked around the house with you, around and around, through the grass, past the back door, through the grass, past the front door, carrying you and showing you all the wonderful things that were outside. Your mother said, 'Look up at the moon. It makes everything bright.' "

She wiggles on my lap. "Now say what I said."

"You looked at the moon and then you said, 'The moon is the door to God's house.' "

She looks at me. "Did I say that?"

"Yes."

"Is it?"

"If you say so."

"I do. And I wasn't afraid of the dark anymore?"

"Were you?"

She laughs. "Only sometimes."

I hold her close. *It's all right*, I think. *We're all afraid of the dark sometimes.*

After kissing everyone, Jennifer goes to bed. We take turns tucking her in, singing to her. We turn on her night light. Finally we hear her singing to her doll. Soon it is quiet. I savor these moments when we are together again under this strong, sheltering roof, beside this comfortable hearth. I am deeply aware of our good fortune, of the warmth of our lives together.

Jerry stays with Jennifer while the rest of us go to the midnight service at St. Paul's. Once again Todd and I with our daughters come to this fragrant, candle-lit church. We wait together, part of a Christian community poised on the edge of mystery, in expectation of a drama that unfolds year after turning year.

Together with my family, centered on silence, filled with thanksgiving, I wait for the Holy Birth, the healing, life-giving miracle of love.

CHAPTER
FORTY

Christmas was over, the new year was almost a month old, and it had been raining for weeks. We southern Californians are not used to so much rain, and neither is our soil.

"I'm beginning to feel like Mrs. Noah," I said as Todd and I and Alice stared out at the water that rushed down the street in front of our house, carrying with it stones and twigs from the hill above.

"What a night," Alice said. "I'm glad I'm only going across the street." She slipped into her raincoat and pulled up the hood. "Well, stay dry," she said. "Pleasant dreams."

Alice's friend, Becky, was nervous about being alone while her parents spent a few days in Mexico, so Alice had arranged to stay there at night until Becky's parents returned.

In all our years in this secluded canyon home of ours we had never seen such rain. "Look at that," I said. "I just can't believe it." Now the water flowing down the road carried with it small boulders and whole branches from the wooded area to the north. "Will our hill hold?" I asked Todd.

"I hope so. I hope all the hills hold." I knew he was thinking of our neighbors, all as vulnerable as we were.

At about midnight we went to bed. Despite our apprehension, we had been fascinated by this display of nature on the move, but we were tired.

Our bedroom was separated from the rest of the house by a concrete-walled breezeway. The dog slept on a mat outside our door and that night she whimpered, restless. Once I got up and looked out to see the rain driving, slanting, relentless. Finally I slept.

We were awakened by a crash.

For a moment we lay, stunned with sleep. Then Todd said, "I think one of the big oaks must have fallen." He hurried out of bed and I stepped into my slippers and followed him, flinging on a robe.

It all happened in seconds, but it had the feeling of a slow-motion film.

Todd opened our bedroom door and stepped into the breezeway.

With a crash both the breezeway doors fell in.

The dog dashed outside.

Todd cried, "Hurry!" and held out his hand to me.

We stepped inside the kitchen just before a tidal wave of mud swept through the space between our bedroom and the house, knocking down the concrete wall, blocking the door to our room.

Standing in the kitchen, we looked through the window into what had been our den. Mud met our gaze, on eye level. The entire room was under mud. Two things were visible: a lamp, hanging from the ceiling over the spot where my desk should be, and a clock, its hands stopped at five minutes of five. The crash had been the collapse of the den.

Speechless, numb, we ran down the hall to the other bedrooms. The room where Alice would have been sleeping was unrecognizable, her bed buried under five feet of plaster and mud. The heavy beam roof and a part of the wall were all that remained. Muddy water flowed through the room that Alice was using as a study. One wall had caved in. The room was full of smoke.

Todd and I looked at each other. Finally I said, "Alice is safe. We're all safe." We clung to each other. That was the moment from which we drew the strength we needed for the ordeal ahead. Our home had been destroyed, but our lives had been spared. We had each other.

We began to move through a nightmare. A tide of flowing mud has enormous strength, and we fought it. We fought time. We fought the elements as they conspired against us.

Throughout our nightmare in the hours, days, and months ahead, we would seek each other's eyes, reach out to touch each other, for we knew that we saw and touched the important reality. We were still a family.

First, that morning, I telephoned Alice across the street. The girls had been awakened by the crash. "The house has fallen in," I told her. "You'd better come home."

"Call the fire department," Todd said to me, "and the police. Ask if they can give us some help." The smoke in the rear of the house was increasing.

I called the fire department first. "Our house has fallen in," I told the dispatcher. Even as I spoke I thought, *How ridiculous this sounds.* "And we're on fire."

The rain was violent. "Are you sure there's a fire?" the dispatcher asked me.

"Well, there's smoke," I insisted.

The firemen discovered that the fire was in the bedding. A short circuit had ignited the gas from a displaced wall heater. Alice would have been in that bed.

Both the firemen and the police did more than their routine work that dark morning. Alice, rushing barefoot through all that mud and water, was trying to rescue her books.

"Young lady, get out of there," said a fireman. "We don't want you to be electrocuted. And this outer wall may go at any time."

"But my books," she protested.

So he cut the wires and helped her carry loads of books into the dining room.

Still in my night clothes, I knew that I had to be dressed more warmly and practically. Todd had torn off the screen to our bedroom window. He had climbed through the window and dressed in the dark. Over the protests of the firemen, I did the same.

"Hurry," the man called to me. "We don't know whether the wall will hold."

I made two more calls, thankful that the telephone still worked. The first call was to one of our parish clergy. The next was to one of my husband's business associates.

Help came within minutes. Friends from St. Paul's arrived with trucks and packing boxes.

Men from the office came with shovels. As people arrived to help, they began to dig. Hundreds of shovels full of mud were moved that first day. And during the following days we literally moved mountains, partly, one might say, by faith.

We shoveled beside friends and strangers, people of all ages. Long-haired, bearded boys dug beside girls in blue jeans. Some of them we had never seen before, and where they came from, we never knew. Coffee and sandwiches appeared. We fed multitudes with food sent to us from what we now thought of as the outside world. Loaves and fishes.

By the end of that first interminable day we thought that most of the immediate danger to the house had been relieved. The police promised to patrol during the night and call us if further trouble threatened. Neighbors took us in just as we were: muddy, cold, exhausted.

We called Meg in the Northwest and told her what had happened.

Horrified, she asked, "Do you want me to come?"

I had to laugh. "Your room's gone. There's no place to put you. But we're all fine."

I heard the tears in her voice as she said, "I'm glad I finally took my wedding dress with me at Christmas. It would have been in that closet."

The next morning I went to St. Paul's to perform my duties as choir director. I wore the only clothes I had at hand, the ones I had taken off. I put on my muddy slacks, shirt and tennis shoes. We didn't know, then, where our clothes were. We found them later at the church, spread out in the parish hall, like a rummage sale.

Long choir robes cover anything, and my dirty clothes didn't show that Sunday morning. I teetered between laughter and tears during the entire service. There was a merging of the solemn and the ridiculous.

Alice and I, standing opposite each other in the choir stalls, hardly dared meet each other's eyes. Everything seemed to be directed at us. Psalm 66 tells of people going through the flood on foot.

Sure enough, Alice's eyes laughed at me, *we went through fire and water.*

And sure enough, I thought back at her, *we came out again into a safe place.*

In the midst of our church family that morning we felt upheld by love and caring. And we learned more about such love during the weeks that followed. The spontaneous gestures of goodness and generosity did not end after the initial impact of our disaster.

Friends loaned us the apartment they had prepared to rent, telling us to use it as long as we needed it.

Parish families brought us our meals. Each day after working in the mud, in that cold rain that would not stop, we went to our warm apartment and were greeted by people bringing us a hot meal, sometimes embellished with flowers and candles.

Nothing was too large or too small for people to do for us. Friends did our unspeakably muddy laundry. And we were especially moved by an envelope that came to us. It contained pennies, nickels, a few dimes: a gift from some children who had heard about our trouble and just wanted to help.

Todd and I had come to middle age. We had been through all the usual expenses of raising a family. Our house was nearly paid for. We had begun to plan for the European trip that we had always promised ourselves.

One rush of mud buried our security and our dreams.

But I can honestly say that none of it mattered.

A few months later on a spring day when the sun shone and the breeze was dry and warm, we gave a party. Our guests were people who had helped us put our lives together again.

"Well," one of the boys said, "this is a real switch from last time I was here."

We stood together in the new back room. It is beautiful, cheery and bright, and it looks out on a concrete retaining wall that must surely be one of the strongest in California. This boy had helped build it.

"It's a real winner." He grinned at me.

"That it is," I agreed.

Another friend, inspecting the garage, saw the clock with its hands pointing to five minutes of five. "You kept it," she said.

"Yes. Somehow I wanted to."

"I think I know how you feel," my friend said. "But aren't you glad it's over?"

It isn't over. Not all of it.

Part of that day, the day the hill came down, will always stay with us. The clock reminds us of it. Time may seem to stop, one's life may seem to be impossibly altered. But it is possible, despite catastrophe, that something else will begin. Something warm and sustaining and beyond price.

CHAPTER
FORTY • ONE

—————————— ❧ ——————————

"**J**ulie, you're going to lose your wedding ring one of these days." My friend Eleanor sounded concerned but also somewhat amused.

Startled, I looked at the ring, a plain narrow circlet of gold. It had worn so thin that it did, indeed, look near the breaking point. I had not realized how fragile it was and I was alarmed at the thought of losing it.

"I'll take it to the jeweler," I told Eleanor. "Maybe he can strengthen it somehow."

"Why don't you just ask Todd for a new one? That's what I did. When we were married we couldn't afford much in the way of rings, either." She glanced at my modest engagement ring and the wedding band, precariously circling my finger. "So Fred got new ones for me when we could afford them." She held out her hand and I saw the blaze of diamond fire, the sleek platinum bands. I thought of Celia and her diamond ring so long ago.

But I didn't want new rings. Mine had been blessed at our marriage. I'd worn them for thirty-five years. They were as much a part of me as the skin of my fingers.

The jeweler was able to strengthen the gold somehow. I was too relieved to ask questions. "They're good for another decade or so, Mrs. Ashton," he told me.

And so are we, I said to myself, *God willing*.

I thought of our wedding, Todd's and mine, that wartime year. The church had been especially beautiful with sunlight filtering through stained glass, with white chrysanthemums on the altar, with Bach, majestic and solemn, pouring from the organ.

I thought of Meg's wedding, too, years later at St. Paul's. It had followed the same proper rubrics. Todd and I had assumed that her marriage, like ours, would endure forever.

So we were profoundly shaken when Meg called one night from her home in Washington to tell us that after ten years her marriage was over. Our son-in-law had moved out, the house was to be sold, the dissolution of the marriage was legally underway. She sounded sad but controlled.

Jennifer was subdued and withdrawn when she spoke to us. "Daddy isn't going to live with us anymore," she said, her voice forlorn.

We felt helpless. I was almost glad my mother was not alive to bear this anguish.

Then, very quickly, we thought, after only a few months Meg called us joyfully. "I'm in love," she said. "He's wonderful. You'll love him, too. We're living together. This time I want to be perfectly sure. I've explained it to Jennifer. She understands."

Understands? Our tradition says that you don't live with a man unless you are married to him. Especially not with a six-year-old daughter. Todd and I grieved. Uneasily we received them in our home at Christmas. The three of them.

There had never been a divorce in our family and never a situation like this one. Tradition said, *Not in this house. Not unless you are married.*

Love said, *You are adults. We don't have to approve. We won't judge. But we love you. We want you. Come.*

It was a strange Christmas. But we were together: Todd and I. Alice. Meg and Garth and Jennifer.

Oh Come, All Ye Faithful.

And then, in the spring, came another call. "We're going to be married at the end of the summer. We want you to come."

So we went to Meg's wedding. Again. This time a thousand miles away, in the Pacific Northwest.

The bride and bridegroom got up early on the wedding day. We all did. Together we prepared a pre-wedding feast for friends who were coming: men, women, assorted children. And after the meal we all went to the marriage place together.

Meg, serene in a pale green dress, carried a bunch of garden flowers one of the children had gathered for her. Jennifer led the way, with two of her friends, and all of us, friends and strangers, walked from the house down the hill to the edge of Puget Sound. A fine mist veiled grass and shrubs. Under a huge tree musician friends played baroque music on baroque instruments. We grouped around our daughter and her man. There, under the tree, in the soft rain, at the edge of the water, they were married.

The young minister wore slacks and a pullover sweater. The marriage service was a mixture of rites: words from the Book of Common Prayer, from the Wedding Book, words of their own.

A goldsmith had made the wedding rings in a design of interlocking circles, and he had made a pendant for Jennifer using the same design. As part of the ceremony our daughter clasped the pendant around her daughter's neck, the three of them joined hands, and the minister pronounced them a new family. Then he blessed them. So did we all.

Tradition? Webster says that originally it meant a betrayal, a delivering into enemy hands. For a while I thought I would have to consider this new tradition in those terms.

But I have come to believe that Tradition may sometimes be fluid when it is created with love, when it is shared. Our daughter and her family have given us such a gift.

Now we pray for a golden circle of love, a holy circle that will enclose them all, binding them together with power and lasting beauty, even when it has worn thin.

CHAPTER

FORTY • TWO

A dvent is the season in which we prepare ourselves for the coming of Christmas, the arrival of Christ in our lives. To be sure, ideally we know that the Christ is with us and we with him not only at the time of the mystic Birth, but always. But Advent is a yearly reminder of our need to prepare a welcome, to ready ourselves, our souls, to receive this Holy Child.

One year, all during Advent, I could not throw off my grief at my continued estrangement from Martin. He was constantly in my mind, in my heart. And Todd and I grappled with a sadness that we knew was selfish, but that we could not throw off.

For the first time in years our family would be separated at Christmas. Alice, living at home near her work at the hospital, would be with us, but the others would not.

Under the legalities of Meg's divorce it was arranged that Jennifer would spend one Christmas with her mother, the next with her father. On this particular year she was to be with Jerry. Meg and Garth were to spend the holiday sailing with friends among the San Juan islands.

"I'm really sorry," Meg told us on the telephone. "We'll miss being with you. But we're excited about this trip, and we'll plan to be with you next year, the three of us."

When we spoke to Jennifer her voice was sad. "I can't go with Mommy and Garth," she said. "And I can't come to see you." Her tone brightened. "But I'll be with Daddy and my other Nana."

Todd and I had been trying, all during Advent, to prepare ourselves for those vacancies.

"I am sure that I could keep Christmas no matter what," a friend told us when we shared our sadness with her. "I could keep Christmas alone in a hotel room in a strange city. Christmas does not depend upon the externals. It is a state of mind."

I know she is right. And yet . . . that seems so austere. What about the memories? The traditions? The small sacraments of family love that surround this blessed time?

Even as I write this, I am thrown back to that Advent time, the time from which I learned so much. I live it all again, feel the pain and the sense of loss.

❋ ❋ ❋

As I prepare for the holy night, I try to hallow tasks, small and large. We bake cookies to send to Meg, Garth, and Jennifer so that they may enjoy them together before Jennifer leaves to be with her father.

"What do you want me to make for you?" I ask when I talk to them on the phone.

Jennifer's answer comes at once. "Santas and trees and stars and bells."

I find myself praying over the cookies as I roll and cut, bake and decorate them. *Let them be a sign of love , a symbol of joy.*

Tears come when I least expect them: in the grocery store when I see a woman my age happily shopping with a five-year-old; when Musak in a department store blares out "Deck the Halls"; and when in church we pray for those whom we love, parted from us by distance.

Todd and I observe all the rites and customs. We get the Christmas tree and decorate it. We plan a festive meal, inviting friends who would otherwise be alone. But something in me cringes. Our circle will not be complete.

Christmas Eve arrives, and with it a severe storm. Wind rages, power lines are down, the lights go out. Our friends telephone to say they cannot come to be with us after all.

And Alice comes home from the hospital white and drawn. I know that something terrible has happened. She goes into her room. After a while I follow.

She is sitting on the edge of her bed, not moving, not weeping. I sit beside her. "Can you tell me?" I ask, finally.

Her voice is flat as she says, "Sometimes I think I can't stand it."

I wait, knowing that she will tell me when she can.

"If only she hadn't died today, this afternoon, Christmas Eve."

"Who?" I ask her. "Who died?"

"My open-heart surgery patient. Maria. She was seventeen. I had to tell her parents. The doctor said he couldn't face telling them. Not on Christmas Eve. So he asked me to tell them. They barely understood English, but they understood what I was telling them." Alice's eyes were dark with agony.

I put my arms around her and she leans against me as she used to do when she was a child. "I'm so sorry," I tell her, "so terribly sorry."

Todd comes into the room. "Are you all right?" he asks Alice.

She sighs and tells him what has happened. He sits beside her, too, and the three of us are linked by pain. Pain for the parents who have lost a child on this night, our own pain at the absence of those we love. But even as I grieve, I know that my grief is nothing compared to that of the parents who have lost their daughter.

"That isn't all," Alice said. "I waited until the priest came and he told them it was God's will. He said they had to accept it because it was God's will. I don't believe it. I don't think God wanted Maria to die. He wanted her to get well and live out her life. I think God is sad, too."

I believe that. I cannot believe that a loving God wills these tragedies. Surely he does not. But somehow we have to learn to live with grief. And tonight I am not sure that I know how.

Our usually festive dinner is subdued this Christmas Eve. We think of loss. Meg without Jennifer. Jennifer without her mother, away from us. And Maria's parents, crushed and desolate.

We go to the late service at St. Paul's. The candles are lighted, the air redolent with pine, the music almost unbearably beautiful. The three of us are joined in our pain and our heaviness.

How can we welcome a birth in the midst of separation and death? What meaning can this night have for us now?

I feel alien, alone, although I am with two beloved people. There is so much trouble, unrest, hatred in this world of ours. We have come so far from Eden. How long will God have patience with us? How long will the Son come among us, into the messes we make of our lives, into a world that we have nearly ruined with our greed? Merry Christmas?

I try to pray.

Gradually, there in the hush of candlelight, among the members of this Christian family, a sense of peace begins to invade me. God sent . . . God sends . . . his Son precisely because we need him now, more than ever. We don't earn that gift, that Coming. It is through the abundance of God's grace that the gift is given. Over and over and over. We can believe and trust. No matter what. That is the true Christmas gift: the unearned gift of peace, of peace past our understanding.

CHAPTER
FORTY · THREE

—————— ❦ ——————

When I was a child I tried to understand the things my father said about Easter. "Only when we live through the darkness of Lent and Good Friday can we truly celebrate Easter," he said. "The light of Easter means nothing without knowledge of the darkness that precedes it."

Martin and I gave up things we really liked as part of our preparation for Easter. We put money we would have spent on candy and movies in our Mite boxes. I was always a bit vague about what actually became of the money we dropped through the slot into those blue boxes. I hoped that the people who finally used it appreciated what we had done for them.

I knew Easter was inevitable. On that morning we would sing my favorite hymns. In our Sunday school classes we would be given crosses made of chocolate, filled with thick vanilla cream and decorated with flowers. I hoped the sugar flowers on my cross would be pink, not blue. And then, the next Saturday we would go to the movies.

When I mentioned these things to my father he seemed to be disappointed. "I have failed you," he said. "You are, after all, too young to understand."

How very distant those childish concerns are now. My poor Father, if indeed you failed us, it was because you were so caught in your own darkness that you could not show us the way into light.

I wondered, this Lent, whether I would be able to find a way out of the darkness under which Todd and I had been walking. When Todd returned from a medical examination one day early in Lent he came into the living room and sat in his own chair. For a while he looked at me without speaking. The silence was heavy. I read it, knowing him so well, and went to kneel beside his chair, to take his hand.

"It's bad," he said. "It's malignant."

Malignant: actively evil in nature; highly injurious; threatening to life or health.

When one walks with a malignancy, one walks in the shadow, and that shadow is shared by those who care. Never had we felt so firmly supported by family and friends as during this time of our deep need. Our rector and the parish upheld us. We asked the prayers of those friends distant from us whom we knew to be strong in prayer.

One of these special friends wrote, "I read recently that when you are praying for healing you should not think of the person as being ill, but as whole and healed, praising God for the healing. So I shall see him whole and healthy as I pray.

"*Whole, heal, healthy, holy,* all spring from the root word 'hale,' as in hale and hearty. So I shall pray for his healing and wholing and holiness."

Throughout Lent I tried to hold this vision of Todd. He underwent radiation therapy in preparation for surgery, scheduled soon after Easter. Between treatments he worked in the yard, in the house, calmly going about his ordinary tasks.

I wrote to Martin about Todd's illness, but I did not hear from him. When Todd and I went to St. Paul's at noon on Good Friday I felt as I had when I was a child, that Easter might never come. That Good Friday would last forever. I found it difficult to center myself on the words of the liturgy. I was trying to deal with the fear that hung over me.

Then, during one of the periods of silence for meditation, a memory gradually came into my mind, the memory of a day in Florence. Todd and I were in the church of Santa Maria Novella. On one wall, looming out of the shadows of that great basilica is a fresco by Masaccio. It is called *The Holy Trinity.*

Christ is there, crucified. Behind him, supporting the cross, bearing the same weight, sharing the pain, is God the Father. His eyes look into ours with understanding and compassion, with forgiveness and love.

Remembering those eyes, I offered up this dark Good Friday, Todd's and mine, in acceptance and in trust, as I leaned toward Easter.

CHAPTER

FORTY · FOUR

———————— 🍇 ————————

On the afternoon of Easter Day Todd and I sat together in the patio under the wisteria vine, a veritable fountain of fragrant lavender blossoms. Large black bees lumbered about, sounding industrious and diligent.

We had been up at dawn to take part in the first Eucharist of Easter. The paschal moon still showed faintly in the morning sky, our town was quiet, and St. Paul's, when we arrived, was festal with white and gold. The air was full of Alleluias. And over and over during the service came the words, "Do not be afraid."

Now Todd and I didn't talk much. We sat companionably, each with private thoughts. I looked at him, studying the familiar face. *He's worn well*, I thought. His face still has the look of kindness and strength that has always marked it. Now those qualities are intensified.

He saw me looking at him. "What are you thinking about?"

I countered with, "I was going to ask you the same thing."

He smiled. "I was remembering the Easters when the girls were little. The baskets of flowers they took to church. The egg hunts after dinner. They were good days, weren't they?"

"Beautiful days," I agreed. And I thought, *But they aren't ending. We'll have more. I know we will.*

Then the doorbell rang and I went to see who was there. It was a special delivery messenger with a package for me. "Sign here, please," he said. "And Happy Easter."

"Thank you. I wish you the same. It's too bad you have to work today."

"Oh, I don't mind. It's pretty out. Kind of special."

I carried the parcel to the patio. Martin's return address was on the outer wrapping but no note was included in the package. Inside was a book bound in cloth with an exotic design of bamboo, beige on rose. The edges of the blank pages were marbled with delicate lines of rose and blue and cream.

Oh Martin, I thought. *You remembered.*

I could see him, a sturdy little boy with blond curls, his hand smoothing the pages of an empty book. I could see him, a quiet, serious man, almost a stranger, carefully selecting this book. This particular book. For me.

And I thought, *There is a chance for us, after all. A new covenant of reconciliation when we will all be healed and whole and holy.*

That night as I thought about the hospital days and nights facing Todd, the anxious days and nights facing me, I wrote the first entry in my journal from Martin. Words from the poet-prophet, Isaiah:

See!
I will not
forget you . . .
I have carved you
on the palm
of my hand.

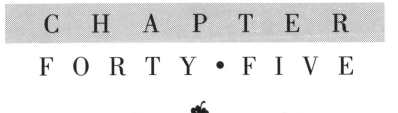

CHAPTER
FORTY • FIVE

A
nd so Todd and I have reaped the harvest that is rich and blessed beyond all desiring. He is well; whole, hale, hearty, holy. And I go about singing aloud and silently, Hosanna! Blessed be the God who has led us through fire and pain into the realm of ineffable calm, through his great mercy.

It is summer again. The rains are over and past, the hills are brown, the deer come down once more seeking water. And we, part of the faithful remnant, still face the problems of the world, great and small. Are we, as a nation, reaping the harvest of past mistakes, of greed and arrogance? New wars have been fought and the desolate aftermath remains. Hostages remain in captivity. Children starve. The nations rage furiously together. The stark face of evil is seen in the land.

And yet, we are not forgotten. The finger of God moves over our lives, and, whether or not we understand, he controls his creation. We try to remember that his is a kingdom of love and that love must be our response. He never told us it would be easy.

On the edge of the precipice, Todd and I prepare to meet whatever comes together, giving thanks for the God who has promised not to forget or forsake us. We are his children, the sheep of his pasture, the fruit of his planting, the frail creatures of his making, inching our ways toward the final harvest that awaits us, secure in the knowledge that we are surrounded by that Love which passes all understanding.

Caryl Porter, a mother and grandmother, lives with her husband in Southern California. Like Julie in the novel, she was a teacher for many years. Her family, her writing, music, and active participation in the life of her church are vitally important to her. She has previously published three novels, and her poems, stories, and articles have appeared in numerous magazines and literary quarterlies. She is presently a music critic for a metropolitan newspaper.